| | | DATE DUE | |
|---|---|---|---|
| | | | |
| | | | |
| | | | |
| | | | |
| | | | |
| | | | |
| | | | |
| | | | |
| | | | |
| | | | |
| | | | |

# SMILE

## AS

## THEY

## BOW

# SMILE
# AS
# THEY
# BOW

A NOVEL

## NU NU YI

TRANSLATED FROM THE BURMESE BY

### ALFRED BIRNBAUM AND
### THI THI AYE

HYPERION

EAST

NEW YORK

Library of Congress Cataloging-in-Publication Data has been applied for.

ISBN-13: 978-1-4013-0337-2

Hyperion books are available for special promotions, premiums,
or corporate training. For details contact Michael Rentas,
Proprietary Markets, Hyperion, 77 West 66th Street, 12th floor,
New York, New York 10023, or call 212-456-0133.

Book design by JoAnne Metsch

FIRST EDITION

10 9 8 7 6 5 4 3 2 1

TO MY
GRANDFATHER
AND
GRANDMOTHER

SMILE

AS

THEY

BOW

## 1

### FIRST
### DAY OF
### OBEYANCES

JUST NOW, A WEEK BEFORE THE AUGUST FULL MOON, an enchanted air lingers over Taungbyon. As festival time draws near, the Mandalay–Madaya turnoff backs up with cars, trucks, buses, and jeeps—and throngs of anxious passengers all in bright colors. A mischievous August breeze plays above the narrow road awash in yellow puddles, spillover from the canal that runs alongside. The soulful monsoon-weather skies have everyone in a festive mood. It's time to be happy and carefree.

Young boys laugh and shout from the roofs of buses while womenfolk, crammed inside, mumble anxious prayers. Well-to-do ladies sitting comfortably in chauffeured sedans raise hands to their foreheads in reverence to the *nats*. Sunburnt children in scruffy clothes along both sides of the road shout, "Throw money! Throw money!" They size up the incoming caravan, faces full of hope, eyes peeled wide for any tossed scrap of paper, then dive in with elbows flying.

Suddenly clouds of dust-choked exhaust wheeze up from braking engines. Alarmed voices cry out as the kids scramble to grab bills from right under the tires, only to resurface all scrapes and bruises, though a glint of fear in their little eyes betrays their daredevil bravado.

But wait, who are these grown-ups shouting alongside the children? A chorus line of drunks is dancing in the middle of the road with eyes squinted and fingers pointed high. And now farm women from the paddy fields rope their headscarves across traffic, clap hands, and shout at the top of their lungs when any car slows down, "Make merit! Throw us money!"

The lines of merrymakers stretch all the way to the village of Taungbyon, now one great big fairground packed with pilgrims and thatched huts. Inbound progress grinds to a halt as each new arrival tries to find a place to park. Cars and jeeps nose toward cleared fields, larger vehicles lurch into an unpaved bus yard.

As soon as people set foot in the village, they can see the golden-umbrella spire of the Wish-Fulfilling Pagoda above the huddled festival stalls, though the tinkling bells are drowned out by the mad cacophony of festivities.

LONG AGO in the eleventh century, during the golden era of Bagan, King Anawrahta had his court nobles bring one brick each to help build this Wish-Fulfilling Pagoda. Yet, come the appointed day, the king's personal favorites, Indian half-caste lieutenants and brothers Shwepyingyi and Shwepyinlei, failed to show. The two rowdy womanizers had neglected their duties, so the king had no choice but to order them punished. Others in court, however, were jealous of the brothers' growing influence and seized the opportunity to have them killed.

Then one day, as the king was boating down the Irrawaddy, the royal barge froze mysteriously midriver and the two murdered brothers appeared. "Faithfully did we serve Your Majesty, but alas, to no avail!" they decried. "This dragon boat shall not move until we have been vindicated." Greatly saddened by their fate, King Anawrahta vested the apparitions with this riverside dominion and built a shrine near his pagoda to honor the Taungbyon Brothers, now become *nats*—spirits who have met tragic "green deaths" in the classic Burmese tradition.

To this day, the pagoda is missing two bricks, and the empty space is gilded—a holy of holies where the multitudes come to pay homage before pushing on to the Brothers' shrine, popularly known as the Grand Palace of the Nats.

ALL OVER Taungbyon, roadside sweets sellers serve slices of cake drizzled with palm sugar and shredded coconut, the aromas melting in the air already thick with shop girls' flowery perfume and heavily scented makeup. Alcohol vendors tack up a dizzying profusion of signs for palm wine and hard cane liquor—*Mandalay Headspin Special, Tipsy-Top, Lil' Miss Gurkha Rum, Punchdrunk Passion, Feelin' Woozy.*

On past the first stalls, a crowd is bottlenecked at a railroad crossing, crushed up against the sliding guardrail that holds people back from the approaching train. A sudden burst of broiling sun bears down on them and the sweat runs off in streams. Even the breeze is repulsed by the hot, perspiring logjam.

As the Mandalay–Madaya northbound slowly creaks into Taungbyon Station—a mere platform with a sign—it's hard to see the train, there are so many people piled on. Crouching on every inch of roof, leaning out the windows, hanging off the running-boards, all shouting and calling to one another at volumes that rival the raucous festivities.

The train now safely clear, the crossing gate opens and the crowd surges ahead again. Though curiously, in that crush of bodies, the boys aren't teasing the girls like in the old days. They don't thrust stuffed dolls at their prospects or sidle up close with familiar propositions—*Wait up, love! What's for supper, honey?* Don't young people know how to flirt anymore? Are times really that bad? At festivals past, hard as things were, the mood was always eye-to-eye and heart-to-heart and spiced with taunts. Now only grandpas doting on their memories seem eager to tease, though their sweet talk has long since soured to other ears.

People stop in their tracks, however, when they hear come-ons from all the trinket sellers. They can't get enough of the costume jewelry stalls aglitter with faux gold and silver. Necklaces, bracelets, earrings and rings, traditional souvenirs that pilgrims take home from Taungbyon—or try on right here. *Necklaces for five kyats, bracelets for four kyats, earrings for four kyats! Yours to buy! Yours to wear!*

Among the customers, glittering like so many fake bracelets and necklaces, are bevies of fake lovelies young and old. *Mein-*

*masha*, beautifully made up and frocked in blouses and *longyis* tucked to one side in female fashion, come from all over Burma and are everywhere here. This is their festival of festivals.

Keep going. On past the food stalls with cassette players blaring. The roar is deafening—is it even music? Speaker after speaker, each louder than the next, vying for customers. Stalls displaying ready-made coconut-and-banana offering baskets. Stalls with rainbows of scarves, cheap to not-so-cheap.

Closer and closer to the shrine, rows of makeshift *natkadaw* huts shimmer with bright decorations. All the gilded *nat* images seem to come to life under the yellow lightbulbs, the altar tables set before them overflowing with elaborate arrangements of fruit, flowers, snacks, cans of beer and bottles of rum, Pepsi and 7-Up. Meanwhile, the spirit wives sit around on red velvet carpets tossing cowrie dice onto round trays, idly showing off their game.

Just look at all the people juggernauting toward the shrine, yet the Grand Palace stands serene amidst the bedlam. Everyone is high on the unmistakable perfume of the tiny jasmine clusters that only bloom this season. Fresh fragrances fill the air: eugenia, roses, justicia blossoms, yellow ginger-lily. Flower stalls all around sell scarf-wrapped bouquets to offer to the Taungbyon Brothers.

Starting today, the First Day of Obeyances, the Brothers receive the bowing masses. All remove their sandals at the base of the shrine—and sink deep into the mud. The ground is slippery wet from so many pilgrims pouring water into the open mouths of the tiger statues that flank the entrance. Before and after paying respects to the Brothers, believers offer food and drink to their mythical wildcat mounts. There are even vendors who sell tiger treats.

Everyone pushes to get ahead of the others and venerate the Brothers face-to-face inside the Grand Palace. There they are, resplendent in their regalia, ear bobs and arm bands, the sculpted gold likenesses of "Exalted Big and Little Brothers" Kodawgyi and Kodawlei on jasmine-wood thrones. Striking manly poses, one knee up and one leg down, right hand balancing a sword on the shoulder with the left arm akimbo, the two images are virtually identical, only the younger brother is a little smaller.

Beside the throne, shrinekeepers descended from King Anawrahta's original servants busily ferry flowers to and from the altar. Pilgrims dare not go home without their *nat*-blessed bouquets, flowers they will keep all year round to ward off danger, boost business, and seal the success of their plans.

Those who come earliest are said to especially please the Brothers and enjoy higher favor, thus first-comers fight for floor space until finally they can sit, haunches on heels, and knees on the mats, raise flower offerings above their heads, and bow to the sacred images.

## 2

### SECOND DAY OF OBEYANCES

THESE FIRST DAYS, BEFORE THE CEREMONIES BEGIN, I come here devotedly, my Lords. Please favor me and look after me. I come to worship every year, my Lords. Please support and guide me and my children and grandchildren and even my great-great-grandchildren. Give me strength and good fortune, my Lords.

GRANDMA SHWE EIN prostrates her tiny body on the floor of the Grand Palace. Her cheeks are hollow, her palms raised in supplication are flat and thin, and her skin is shriveled, though she still paints her wrinkled face with pale *thanakha* paste and adorns her straw-white topknot with jasmine blossoms. She wears a white blouse over a vintage flower-brocade *longyi,* a forever-folded keepsake from the virgin bride she once was, and a yellowing moth-eaten silk prayer scarf around her neck.

Well over eighty, her head is frail and shaky. Her teeth are starting to go, her eyes are hazy. She sees the people around her, but the two Taungbyon Brothers are nothing but blurs. She can't fight her way closer through the crowds.

HOW MANY years does this make, only imagining my Lords' faces when I pray? Dear me, everything's so different from the old days. I remember going right up to look, slow and steady. *That* was worship. But now . . . where did my youth go?

Back then it wasn't crowded like this. I didn't need to push and shove my way to you, my Lords. I'd pay my respects nice and calm, get my flowers blessed and put them in my hair, then sit for hours in your Palace at my leisure. In those days, a person could still bring her lunch basket and eat right here at your feet.

Now your glory is so great, the whole country comes to *ooh* and *ah*. Such offerings! So many worshipers! An old woman has a hard time getting her flowers blessed. Even a longtime devotee like me. But your humble servant will not go home without a single spray of my Lords' flowers. She'll stay anchored at your feet.

Dear Lords, flowers are so expensive these days! In the old days, a branch of flowers was just a quarter of a kyat. Big bunches of eugenia, justicia, jasmine—all for just a quarter! Now they're five kyats a bunch, my Lords. And then only the teeniest little sprig of eugenia or yellow ginger-lily. Who ever hears of justicia anymore? Should I sing them the verse? *How fragrant the tawny justicia blooms of Taungbyon!*

My children say, Mother, you don't have to go to Taungbyon each and every year. You're getting old, Mother, you can pray from home. But I tell them, What do you know? I can't go back on my word to the Brothers. Never, ever. I made a promise to come every year at festival time. Divine wrath is a scary thing. Last year I was sick in bed and couldn't go. So what happens? They send me nothing but nightmares and I don't get well the whole year. Darn it, I say, I have to go and worship.

Well, it was arranged for my grandchildren to accompany me, but they didn't want to go with their decrepit old grandmother. Fine. What's to stop me from going on my own? Just give me a walking stick, that's all I need. Taungbyon is near enough, I told them, just take me to the edge of the village, then come wait there when the sun cools off again. I want to see my old friends while they're still around.

Yes, I'll visit my friends. Easily said, but the old girl has a hard time finding places all by herself. When I was young, I used to know who lived where. But now at festival time, the whole village is covered with shrines. Makes a person bug-eyed.

In the old days, weren't but a few shrines around the Palace. *Natkadaws* didn't build their own shrines or stay more than a week. They paid their respects and they went home. Back then, my Lords' Palace wasn't all fancied up either. Just a little old shrine. Didn't have these fancy folding doors like today.

Nowadays, they build so many shrines. They put up huts and levy fees. And still there's not enough room, so anyone in the village with a patch of ground lets out space to put up huts. Every house has huts, all filled to capacity. They install pumps and charge for bathing. They collect for lodging. All thanks to you, my Lords.

You feed the people, my Lords, you support your village.

For which we're all grateful. Though, mind you, in the old days, before it was a weeklong festival, it wasn't so crowded on the eighth or ninth. Traditionally only locals came to offer flowers and pray as the *natkadaws* rolled in with sacred images loaded on their oxcarts. Trains didn't even start running until the eighth.

Mandalay folk might arrive that day or the ninth. Mostly by cart, breaking for lunch at the Kaba'in Village monastery. They'd cook a meal at the rest houses under the big banyan trees, then head the rest of the way to Taungbyon when the afternoon cooled off.

I still miss all that, indeed I do. My husband, Po Tha Maung, dead so many years now, was the family oxcart driver for the wealthy U Ba Khin household from Mandalay. The great man and his wife both came and asked for *me*, a village girl, to be their trusted servant's wife. After the wedding we came to this very shrine and prayed to the two Brothers. Ah, my poor husband, he wasn't long for this world.

GRANDMA SHWE EIN grips her walking stick and struggles to get up off the palace floor, when she feels a strong, steady hand grab her arm and help her to her feet.

MY LORDS, who can this be?

"Granny, would you like to go out? May I help you?"

Dear me, what a lovely boy! More glory upon boys like you.

THE OLD woman nods with approval as Maung So Lwin swings a quick arm around her. Meanwhile his other hand skillfully goes about its work, probing the pocket under the front flap of her blouse, seeking out an inside pocket sewn to her bodice.

SHIT! NOTHING! A complete waste of time! The old woman's only got small change, nothing but one-kyat notes fastened with a safety pin.

Forget it, Granny. Singles are out-of-date. The *nats* will sneer if you offer anything less than a seventy-five-kyat General Aung San or twenty-five-kyat Lion. You should have jeweled blouse studs like the other biddies. Last festival, I got me a whole slew of gold buttons and gems from oldies like you.

As long as I've been a pickpocket, I've targeted old people. Easy to approach, easy to squeeze. Too easy. One hit and you score big-time. Strike gold and it's top-quality gold. Hit jewels and you get really precious stones.

"MAY YOU be strong and safe from all danger. May you be free from obstacles and impediments. May your every plan succeed ten times over." The old lady intones blessing upon blessing as she totters down the steps.

NO, GRANNY, I don't wanna be safe from danger. I'll pass on strong and free, too. No glorious long life for me. I just wanna pinch something worth my time whenever I work. You look out for me, Kodawgyi and Kodawlei, and I'll come here every festival to pay you respect with interest. Just don't blame me for sniping easy victims.

Like the old saying goes, *Hie yourself to temple and dig turtle eggs on the way*. Pilgrimages and pilfering go together. Praying and scouting for prey.

So far though, no easy targets this year, my Lords. Other years I'd have hit the jackpot on the Mandalay–Madaya train before the festival even started. Gold and silver by the handful. *Natkadaws* on their way to the festival by the train make prime targets. Lucky for me, they're too busy boarding with their *nat* stuff and baskets and boxes. Gay *natkadaws* especially. All I have to do is tease and flatter. One step too close, though, and I'd get more than I bargained for. They'd be hustling me.

Trains at festival time are great. Packed with people standing in the aisles, body-to-body like Siamese twins. You bet it's crowded. Trains are cheaper. Buses run twenty-five or thirty kyats, but the train's only seven or eight. Me, I'm glad people only mind their money when they're buying tickets. They never notice they've boarded a rolling pickpocket trap.

I always stand chest-to-chest with people to make sure whoever I'm up against at least has a gold chain around his or her neck. Women who dress up their jackets are better yet. I just have to cut away at the cloth very gently from the bottom. Good thing dressy buttons are back in style.

Okay, sometimes I do get fooled by fake gold, but villagers are such simple, hardworking folk, any gold necklace or buttons I pinch from them are gonna be the real thing. No telling how I'll make out this year, though. The train was crowded like always, but I didn't see anybody wearing gold. Used to be villagers kept their savings around their necks, but folks today can barely afford earrings, let alone necklaces.

See all these women with bright gold buttons on their jackets? Let's not count our take just yet. I studied up when I was in Yangon. Twelve-kyat fake gold buttons are big this year. Just my luck. Been up and down the train and what do I get? One thin gold chain from some kid. I'm here three days ahead of time and I can't even cover food and offerings.

Enough of this. Starting tomorrow I'll work the Grand Palace. It's the Royal Brothers' Bathing Day, good chance to make lots of money. Tomorrow all those fancy Yangon ladies will be herding in to see the ceremony. Perfect time to grope for necklaces and cut the bulging purses from under their arms.

"MOVE IT! Out of my way! Stop standing there all beady-eyed like a crow. No pretty young things here to spy on. You'll only get yourself pickpocketed."

Maung So Lwin feels a sharp pain in his side as a loutish woman in her thirties pushes past him. She jabs Maung So Lwin with her elbow and shoots him such a ridiculous, irate glance, he almost laughs.

"Yeah, look out for pickpockets!"

"Damn straight. Can't be too careful. They strip you down to bare bones. I can tell you stories. They don't even spare us poor people. Happened to me three or four times on the train. Didn't leave me the money to buy flowers for offering. Had to apologize to the Lords and head back home. Wasn't nothing else I could do."

Ma San Khin raves nonstop, heedless of the pickpocket nearby. Everyone within earshot is a confidant, even those who look down on her shabby clothes and cheap flowers. She doesn't care who takes offense at her ranting and pushing through the crowd. All she cares about is getting right up close to the two Lords. Get in quick, make a quick offering, get her flowers blessed quick—the important thing is to make a good, long wish. She doesn't have money to buy lunch or shop in Taungbyon, just the resolve to come every year even if she's flat broke.

I WOULDN'T lie to you, Lords. I swear as I'm Tuesday-born, I get poorer and poorer every year. I want to dress up my whole family and come before you in a big car, you know, like a Town Ace or Lancer and offer to my Lords long rolls of *longyi* fabric and tins of imported cookies. But for now, it's all this Tuesday-born wife and mother can do to come here with twenty-five kyats. A measly twenty-five kyats, my Lords. One worn-out ten-kyat, two fives, and five ones I was lucky enough to exchange for new bills. I had to tell my kids and husband I had errands nearby, then I rushed over to Thieves' Market Station in south Mandalay and caught the train to Taungbyon.

If my husband finds out I came here, it's gonna be a drag-out fight for sure, my Lords. You know he threatened me: *I'll kill you if you go to Taungbyon this year.* He's no good. Even with the blessings you bestow on us, all our income, we never have anything to show for our efforts because of him, my Lords. He eats that Chinese fatback, which I know you don't like. Not that we can afford to buy meat. He bums it off his friends and eats it right in front of me! Does it just to be mean because I believe in *nats*. Please punish him, my Lords, teach him a lesson. But please, don't let him die, because I'll never get by as a widow with his children to look after.

And please give me a winning sweepstakes number in my dreams, just like you did last year, Lords. Last year, I won one thousand, five hundred kyats, which I invested toward the vegetables I sell. But one thousand, five hundred kyats doesn't last very long, my Lords, because rice keeps going up in price and I have hungry mouths to feed. I had to beg favors of that woman who demands interest paid daily.

You must be tired of hearing my problems over and over again, but now that I've got a load off my chest, my mind is clear of a whole year of worries. That's my Lords' power and my Lords' glory. So please feed us, even just a meal or two. Give me winning numbers for the sweepstakes and the lottery, and on the way home, point out any little sack of gold or money some rich swell may have dropped, my Lords.

MA SAN KHIN looks the two Brothers square in the face, says all she has to say at length, then forces her way out through the crowd, her eyes scouring for gold necklaces or money— any support the two Brothers might send her way.

OH, LOOK, what's that? All those big gold necklaces and gold bracelets and diamond earrings and rings. No, can't take those. Didn't anybody lose them on the Palace floor, some- one's *wearing* all that jewelry. Just look at that rich cow.

I want to be like her, Lords. I wouldn't mind getting fat, if it means eating whatever I like. Look at her smooth, oily skin, the kind of body made for big bold batiks, her thick neck decked in heavy gold necklaces down to her navel, huge wrists layered with gold bracelets, fat fingers stuffed into gemstone rings, ears sparkling with diamonds. They go with those round cheeks made up with red blush, my Lords.

See all the turbans and *longyi* fabric she's offering? I'd happily die to come call on you like her, Lords. It'd be my pleasure. She even brings her own servants, too! Following with her tins of Chinese cookies and fruits, my Lords. Please summon me in style like that woman, O Lords. I need your help quick.

AS THE rich woman and her entourage pass, Ma San Khin breathes in their sweat that reeks of class. Her two gawking eyes almost drop from their sockets. The poor woman thinks Daw Tin Mya Han hasn't a care, not a sesame seed of worry in the world. But as soon as the rich matron sees the two Brothers' faces, tears start to well up. A tragedy the size of Mandalay Hill is melting inside her.

Daw Tin Mya Han hands over her offerings for the Brothers, folded stacks of *longyi* fabrics, cookie tins, and fruits, then after a moment she takes out a handkerchief, paying no attention to the shrinekeeper's pleasantries.

"Is everything all right?"

"Yes, everything's fine."

"Last year you wished for business to prosper, and did it?"

"Yes, it's doing well, thanks to my Lords. Business is very,

very good. That's why I come here now to worship as I promised."

I KEEP the scarves and flowers my Lords blessed; all year long they brought great success in business. Lots of money came in, don't ask how much. But husband in a high position or not, if a wife doesn't know what to do, things just don't go right. Not around him. Not without your help, my Lords. Thanks to you, we have plenty of income to buy a house, cars, and land, but our family life is in a shambles.

DAW TIN MYA HAN touches the corner of her eye with a scented handkerchief. Her jewelry glitters the moment her arms move, then goes still as she presses praying hands to her forehead.

MY LORDS, you already know the mountain of worries in my chest. He . . . he has a mistress, my Lords. A "minor wife," younger than our oldest daughter! What am I to do? In the beginning, at the start of his career, he could hardly stand the smell of alcohol, let alone think about women. He didn't have a clue how to bring in extra money. He was a very simple man, but now he's so clever at everything. Every night he drinks whiskey, then when he's good and primed, he goes to her place. Oh, yes, he's set her up in her own house, my Lords. With a TV!

My words don't reach him anymore. Nor anything my daughters say, my Lords. So I say, I'll tell the *nats* on you. O my

Lords, he used to be so timid and careful not to offend the spirits. Maybe she's cast a spell on him? And do you know what he says? *What's wrong?* he says. *I'm just acting like them.* He says *nats* drink, *nats* have lots of wives. He doesn't realize that nowadays my Lords are observing sabbath vows and not drinking. He doesn't see that you have many wives because you're royalty. I don't want to say it, but only *nats* can have a lot of wives. Who does he think he is? How dare he compare himself to you! Don't let him off easy, punish him! Make him come here, face to the floor at your feet, and apologize. While you're at it, make your little brother have a change of heart and regret the error of his ways. Convince him to leave his mistress.

Meanwhile, there's been talk of a new posting. You have to put a stop to it, Lords. If he's transferred, I can't just pack up and go with him. It'll hurt all of us, my Lords. He says if he moves, I should stay because of my business. As if I don't know he intends to take *her* along with him. He'd take that hussy! That low-class street trash, he puts her first!

When he was promoted to a higher position, I added the syllable "Han" from his name after mine like any respectable wife would, but he said, *Don't embarrass me with your childish pranks.* Yet now he's changed *her* name, given her not one, but two syllables of his name, my Lords. Two.

I suffer, Lords. It gives me pains in my chest, in my stomach. When he was rank and file, I was the one who went without eating just to feed the children. I sold all my jewelry for bribes to get him his post. It hurts me just to think about it, my Lords.

My Lords, you alone can help me. If you get him to break up with his mistress, keep him from being transferred, let the children all pass their examinations, and bring me more success in my business, when things calm down, my Lords, I'll make a huge ceremony for you. I'll put up a three-day pavilion, my Lords.

DAW TIN MYA HAN slowly opens her eyes. The big burning lump of worries in her chest has lightened ever so imperceptibly, but when she tries to stand, her servants have to prop up her bulk.

THEY HAVE to help me to get up because I'm so overweight. And once on my feet, I still can't walk right away. I need to stand awhile, then take slow steps. I've got high blood pressure. Too bad I can't eat snakehead fish now that I can afford it.

Ah, yes, my Lords, I forgot to ask about my own condition. Please keep me in good health, don't let diabetes or heart disease claim me. I want to live a good, long life, over one hundred years with a peaceful mind.

DAW TIN MYA HAN puts her palms together and raises them to her forehead again, then exits slowly, mouthing interminable invocations. Meanwhile on all sides of the shrine hall, countless women, men, and gays hold up flower offerings to their closed eyes and repeat fervent wishes just like hers.

## 3

NIGHT OF
THE GRAND
COUNCIL

IT'S ALMOST TIME FOR THE GRAND COUNCIL TO convene. Sweating under the hot midafternoon sun, pilgrims push their way to the Grand Palace of the Nats where, front and center between statues of the two Taungbyon Brothers, the Chief Celebrant takes his seat. One row back sit the two northern and two southern Queen Mothers, all in their eighties. Behind them kneel the various turban-wearing Ministers, then rows of important shrinekeepers and senior *natkadaws* from all over the country with their *nat* son and daughter devotees.

Everyone is here this first festival day: royalty and officials, guards and swordsmen, gong ringers and regalia bearers, dignitary after dignitary. All must take their sacred positions so that the Chief Celebrant, Queen Mothers, and Ministers may invoke the Seven House Spirits and invite those earliest ascended martyrs to feast. Then, as always, there will be ritual cockfight dancing.

The hereditary palace players wait in readiness. Until they strike up, not a single gong dares sound this Grand Council Day. After tomorrow, four days till the full moon, when the two Taungbyon Brothers are bathed and returned to their throne in the Palace, then every other instrument can play, but not a moment before. That is the tradition. Who would dare disobey? Should any musician transgress, everyone will tell you his days are cursed.

At precisely three o'clock, the lead drummer's hand poised on the smallest drum starts to play an enticing rhythm that animates the whole of Taungbyon. Immediately, all who hear, *natkadaws* in their huts and pilgrims alike, stop whatever they're doing, raise hands to their foreheads, and bow in unison toward the Palace.

A BRIGHT, clear voice issues from a two-story dwelling not far from the Palace.

"After the Triple Gem—Buddha, Dharma, and Sangha— the three objects of veneration we hold most precious, I respectfully pay obeisance to you, Bobogyi and Bobolei, whose prowess, karma, and justice shine transcendent. I touch my head to the ground at your feet.

"I will go to Mahamuni Pagoda in Mandalay and donate the many jewels I've collected expressly for you, my Lords. I shall share out those many blessings so that you Taungbyon Brothers might equally benefit from my meritorious deed. And so that I might become a tenfold benefactor to the pagoda, monastery, and priesthood. Before leaving this world of desires and attachments, may I, too, attain full measure of King Setkyawadei and King Thawka Thiridhamma's greatness as a righteous servant of the Faith and become an adept in the ways of the Dharma.

"Let me be an instrument for my Lords. Let all those born in the shelter of your glory, all seven days of the week, noon and night, Sunday, Monday, Tuesday, Wednesday, Thursday, Friday, and Saturday, be blessed with peace and good health for years to come so as to fulfill your will, my elder Lords. You know I don't partake of alcohol or defile others' wives or ply them with drink in order to wheedle money. Grant me eloquence, let pearls of potency twirl off my tongue, my Lords."

Inside the house, the entire upstairs is laid with brand-new woven bamboo mats bordered in bright red velvet. At the head of the room, before a red carpet, a three-tiered altar is laden with fancy Thai snacks, tins of imported cookies, bowls of fruit, scarves, turbans, and *longyi* fabric. On the top shelf, a sumptuous gilded lacquer offering tray decorated with leaf arabesques bears a solitary sacred object—a *nat* turban. Nowhere is there a single *nat* image, though a Buddha altar with twinkling lights and vases of gladioli presides high on the wall above.

Huddled humbly on the carpet with knees to one side, pale skin and light makeup, hands supplicating in prayer, the supple though hardly willowy figure in his fifties is the famous *natkadaw* U Ba Si—better known as Daisy Bond. He opens his eyes and looks around to see a group of faithful followers kneeling on the mats in reverent awe.

Daisy Bond shines them a smile and says, "Oh, you've arrived! Tell me, when did you leave Yangon? You got here just in time for the Grand Council, did you? 'Course you did! Had to come pay your respects. Did you hear? I was just praying for all of my *nat* children born each day of the week. Come up, come up. What's that you have there?"

Daisy grabs a paper bag one woman holds out to him. "Oh, a scarf! You're offering a scarf! By the merit of this act, from this day forward, your good luck begins! Satisfied?"

"Please pray for my Tuesday-born daughter," says the woman, "so she'll pass the tenth grade this year with honors!"

"We have a Tuesday-born girl, my Lords!" Pressing the scarf to her forehead, Daisy begins to babble an invocation. The woman clasps her hands in prayer and closes her eyes, while several other bejeweled Yangon ladies hand her large bills.

"Yes, my Lords! Feed them! Clothe them! Let your sons and daughters eat their fill. Let them dress in fineries, my Lords! Let their fortunes rise like the tides, so you might call them here to the festival each and every year! Look after them. Keep them safe from harm, coming and going without bumps or scrapes."

His prayer finished, Daisy Bond lowers the money from his forehead and wedges it into the *nat* turban.

"Okay, now let's call *sadhu!* See the gold bulb on the turban and gold band around the offering tray, the rings and necklaces—all over twenty karats! After the festival, I'll go offer them to the Brothers' shrine at the Mahamuni Pagoda in Mandalay! You, my *nat* children, will all reap the merit. So let's praise this generous deed by calling *sadhu*—well done!"

"*Sadhu . . . sadhu . . . sadhu . . .* "

"*Amyaa . . . amyaa . . . amyaa . . .* a thousand times over!"

"Tell me, have you eaten? Don't be polite, go on downstairs and eat. Can't say as I know what we have today, but there should be plenty. Hey, Ahpongyi! The guests will be eating now, okay? Go on, go on, don't wait for me. Go and eat."

"But first, Daisy, about my son," asks one woman. "Will he get that sailor job?"

Then another asks, "Yes, and how about my husband and his transfer?"

"Yes, yes, things are going to go fine. You'll see. I've already sent out prayers and powerful *metta* for you, so don't worry about a thing. Go on now, go and eat."

Daisy Bond holds his chest and heaves a sigh as he watches the women in their fineries descend the stairs to eat. Exhausted, he downs a glass of tea, then lies down on the carpet with his head on a rattan pillow.

REALLY, he sighs. I'm so tired! People wonder what's so tiring about wearing dresses and flowers and makeup just to sit around and talk.

*Amele!* Talking's a curse. It's been talk, talk, talk since morning. So many different *nats* possessed me, I was frothing at the mouth from talking so much. People all want money. And the more froth I spew, the more money I get. But Daisy Bond has her pride. If I don't want to do something, I don't. I refuse. I just go somewhere and lie down. Even when I was young, if I was tired and somebody nagged me, *Tell me about my son, tell me about my husband,* I'd shout, *Enough! I'm all*

*talked out. Here's your damn money back! I came to Taungbyon for*
*fun and sex!*

I've always been brutally honest. Call Daisy Bond a foul-
mouthed shit, call me what you will. I never used to spout
this *Go-and-eat-now* sweet talk or act possessed when I didn't
feel like it. I may be getting old, but I know a thing or two
about Vipassana meditation. I don't need to flatter people for
money. I'm happy as I am. If I'm true to myself, people will
come to me. Talking too much just means lying.

This spirit-wife life runs us around the pot of hell. True or
false, we have to talk for a living. We deal in lies and pushing
people to offer animals. This many fish, that many chickens
and roosters. Which comes down to *panatipata*—taking lives.

Yes, my Lords, I owe everything to you, yet others speak ill
of me. I tell the truth about us spirit wives, our suicidal
*natkadaw* lot. And they hate me for it—so what? I tell it like it
is. Damn well better believe I do. I've done this too many
years to lie.

Other *natkadaws* don't understand why I call you my Elder
Lords Bobogyi and Bobolei instead of Brothers Kodawgyi and
Kodawlei like everybody else. They say, *Madame Bond invents*
*names just for show. She makes up her own rules.* They don't know
their *nat* history—believe it or not, my Lords! Madame Bond
does not make things up. Unlike them, I've studied. I know
how *nats* first appeared in Bagan during King Anawrahta's
time, then flourished in the Ava, Konbaung, and Yatanabon
periods. Bobogyi and Bobolei must be quite old by now.
I'm sure they're observing precepts and not drinking palm
wine anymore. Which is why I offer only soft drinks. Oh,

yes, Daisy Bond earns her living in keeping with true *nat* lore.

*Amele!* Still the gossip comes. *An old pro like her? A Grand Palace bigshot no less, and not one* nat *image? Scandalous! Is that proper respect for the* nats*? Is she really a* natkadaw*? Is she really a senior Minister?* This, that, and the other thing. . . .

"Hey, I don't need *nat* images! You hear me? Their aura's all I need!"

I don't want *nat* pictures. You won't see a single one in my place. Their power is the main thing, the aura of the two Royal Brothers, the aura of the Thirty-Seven Nats. Keeping their aura in your heart, in your mind, that's the important thing.

See that turban? It's for Lord Mahagiri, the main house guardian spirit. An antique turban bestowed by King Mindon himself and a very rare item, let me tell you. Decorated with old lacquer and real gold and gems. I was meant to have it. People nowadays, all they know is *turban, turban, turban. Offer the* nats *a turban.* So they tart something up by themselves or order one of those chintzy sequined numbers.

Well, this is a *real* turban that came to me by way of that gangster Lanmadaw Hpotok, or actually his wife who has *nat* karma. Anyway, it was destined for me because on the very day I bought myself a new turban, they showed up to sell me theirs. Like I understood antiques. I said, *Why should I buy that? I already have a shiny, brand-new disco turban. I don't want to spend more money.* But a close friend who knows his antiques said, *Buy it. It's an antique, it'll become more precious as time goes by.* So okay, I bought it. I repaired it with real gold leaf and replaced real stones in the settings. I had a gold lacquer altar stand order-made for it. The other new turban I wear to *nat* ceremonies; my disco turban is for dancing.

That antique turban is the only thing I keep on my altar. Nothing else, no *nat* images, no statues at all. And you see? My faithful *nat* sons and daughters don't fall off. No, they come in droves, more and more every year. That's because I've got the aura.

Yes! That leaves Madame Bond free to go up to Putao or to England, to Taungbyon and Yatanagu, wherever and whenever she pleases without all those baskets full of *nat* images. All I have to carry is the one turban in the special foreign-made case I bought for it. I travel the whole country dancing at *nat* ceremonies and the only things on my *nat* altar are trays of bananas and coconuts arranged in the proper places.

Though I still haul all my clothes chests around when I travel. *Amele!* I do love to be beautiful. Nothing but the best, I wear quality. Oh, the pricey dance tunics I have! Even nationally recognized *anyeint* actresses have nothing of the kind. Daisy Bond puts rubies on her *longyis*, I'll have you know. Loose gems from Mogok weren't so expensive in the old days, so I really laid on the rubies and pearls and sapphires.

When I first came to Taungbyon, I just wanted to dress up like a woman. In my hometown, gay or not, I had to look like a man. No fancy stuff, don't even think about it. But when I heard about the boys in Taungbyon, how they dressed and put on makeup whenever they pleased, all very happy and, well, gay, I just had to go see this Taungbyon for myself. I wasn't a *natkadaw* then, didn't know a thing about *nats*. Must have been my female hormones, I just wanted to doll up and dance—and have a boyfriend! To have every young man in sight fall in love with me.

*Amele!* I don't have to tell you. No boy could resist me. When I was young, I was hot stuff. One look at me, they'd be introducing themselves and sweet-talking me.

I still remember the first time I came to Taungbyon. At Yangon Station, while the other *natkadaws* were busy with their belongings, I grabbed up my satchel and took myself a little walk back and forth. In masculine form for the most part, though I had on a slinky green coat and makeup with my long hair in a topknot. After just two passes along the platform, some character ambles up asking, *So which* zat *troupe do you act in?* Oh *dokka!* What a pain! Probably some theater tout, he says, *You must come to Moulmein right away and dance, I'll give you lead billing.* And he starts quoting me how much he can pay per night. *Amele!* Well, you know me, I play it cool like a real actor, when suddenly my sisters are there shouting, *Come on, girl! What're you doing? The train's about to leave! Move your fucking ass!* I swear the guy's jaw just about fell off. My secret out, you better believe I beat a quick exit.

What a trip that was! We were shouting and dancing and eating nonstop, buying snacks at every station. Everything was so cheap back then. The train fare from Yangon to Mandalay was only seven-and-a-quarter kyats. In the old days, you could go from Mandalay to Taungbyon by the Shwetachaung Canal. It was such fun to travel by water, passengers in different boats joking with one another. Such teasing, *Hey, Mama! Where to, Miss? Who's your brother-in-law?* Mind you, the worse they razzed, the more I liked it. If a young man called out, *Hey, sweetheart!* I'd just trill back, *Yes, darling?* But if the drunks got too crude, I'd heap on the abuse.

When we got to Taungbyon, I couldn't control myself, the freedom was almost too much for me. I wore red, top to bottom; I sat in the tea shops with my red headscarf. There were so many *meinmasha* like me there, all making merry with their lads. We all went around freely, dressed like women. First thing in the morning, we'd do ourselves up and step out to the Grand Palace to go "iron gate dancing."

By tradition, when the Palace gates shut after the Grand Council, everyone in the whole village dances out front. The Palace orchestra plays, provided you pay. In the old days, you could request a tune for twenty-five or fifty pyas, half a kyat. Back when one gold sovereign was twelve kyats, two kyats was the most anyone ever paid for a song—and two kyats bought a whole roll of Padma organdy from India *plus* a big can of cooking oil. Nowadays requests can go as high as forty-five or ninety kyats.

With so many people dancing at the gates, we'd all mix with our lads. If anybody complained, my fists were ready for fighting and I'd let 'em have it. Come night and a change into evening clothes, we'd go out dancing again. All night long, from one place to another. It was the happiest time of my life.

The following year, a swarm of cops descended on Taungbyon and rounded up us gays, no questions asked. They didn't take anyone who looked clean-cut or manly. But act swishy, dressed straight or not, well, you went right to jail. Word of the arrests spread. Women *natkadaws* near my hut said, *Don't go out and do something stupid or they'll nab you for sure.* I sat at home in a snit, just dying to make trouble. But how? I couldn't stay cooped up, and I didn't want to look like a man. Finally I rebelled: *Get out there, girl!* I put on women's clothing over a man's *longyi*, with only a touch of makeup, and I step out.

Well, there's a policeman waiting by the Grand Palace. He sees me and says, *You can queer around outside the Palace, but don't go in.* Nice enough, I guess, but the whole thing was I *wanted* to go into the Palace, I *wanted* to make a scene. So when the cop's not looking, I duck in through the side and start acting up. It doesn't take long for him to notice and he storms in to get me. *Just you try,* I think. *Watch this!* In a flash, I strip off my woman's skirt, fold it 'neath my arm, straighten the *longyi* underneath, then I run over to a bystander and borrow his jacket. *Gimme that,* I say. *You'll get it back later.* Presto, I'm out of there, right under the cop's nose, proud of my little performance.

Still, with most of my gay friends in jail, I was bored and lonely. I felt humiliated. Why didn't they arrest me, too? Wasn't I gay enough for them?

I did what I had to. Orange top to bottom, orange scarf on my head, I strutted up and down twirling a handbag and mouthing off. *Hi, boys, I'm gay. Look at me, I walk anywhere I please. I'm not afraid of you bullies.* So of course, they were obliged to arrest me. I got to see my friends in jail and we all had a good time inside.

Well, the very next day, Mae Myint comes to jail to vouch for us. The big queen's even wearing a man's jacket and *longyi. How nice,* I think. *Acting straight today, are we?* So I start shouting, *He's gay too, you know. Mae Myint's really queer. Arrest him, arrest him.* So they did.

I squealed on everyone, not just Mae Myint. I told them who was gay and hiding out at what monastery or in whose house where. I caused such a commotion, soon all the *mein-mashas* in Taungbyon were in jail. But what happened was, it got too crowded. We bitched and fought and swore. We cried. Finally, the police couldn't stand it. They said, *Will Your Ladyships please not make such a racket? You're free to go, but don't stay at the festival. Just go back wherever you came from!*

Most went home peacefully, but I wouldn't dream of it. I hung out in Mandalay with a friend. One night we went with two guys to visit Manthida Gardens by the Mandalay Palace moat. I sat down in one place, and my friend sat down near the Mingala Bridge. I still remember that night. We were both wearing formal white *acheik* skirts and high heels, huge dahlias in our hair.

Sure enough, police came. We were only chatting, but when one cop said, *Come along, dearie,* I hit him and kicked him and ran over to my friend. I was still telling him about how I fought back when I noticed, *Uh-oh, that damn cop's right behind me.* So on the spur of the moment, I slipped off my high heels, jumped up and whacked them in his fucking face, then jumped in the moat and swam across to the other side. When I pulled myself up on the far bank, my *acheik* skirt was gone. I was cold and shaking, with nothing on but my underpants. I must have dropped my dahlia somewhere in the scuffle too. My poor friend was arrested, but I managed to escape. Word of my little escapade spread among the gay community.

*She showed her stuff. She was so brave, a hero for us gays*—and be-cause James Bond movies were just becoming popular in Burma, *Miss James Bond, that's who she is.*

And so Daisy Bond was born. By the time I became a *natkadaw*, no one ever called me anything else. My real name, U Ba Si, all but disappeared.

It's not like I had a choice to become a *natkadaw* or not. This girl, let me tell you, she loves to dress up and dance. As soon as I set foot in Taungbyon, that *nat* blood, that *nat* spirit was in me. How could I see all the trance dancing and not picture myself possessed? Our Miss Bond is a quick study, is she not?

I can't tell you how much the Taungbyon Brothers loved me. Bobogyi and Bobolei made me the super popular Daisy Bond I am today. All my uncles and aunts from good families in Lower Burma doted on me too. They were so happy to hear their nephew was now a spirit bride, I became *their* natkadaw. *Do us some séances*, they'd say. *Here's money for costumes. Be sure to wear expensive dresses. Don't buy fake jewelry or people will look down on you.* The whole deal.

The relatives all came to Taungbyon every year for the festival. They threw birthday parties in Taungbyon too. With cake and ice cream, things country folk here had never seen before. Such a scene. They bought me whole sacks of rice and cooking oil by the can, enough for all my followers these seven festival days. They said I should be more choosy about my circumstances—I shouldn't be sleeping on a bamboo floor in a tiny hut with no toilet, no this or that. Why didn't I buy a house and land in Taungbyon? They'd come with me to put down money and I could pay them back whenever. I couldn't have asked for more. When I got this place, it was only five thousand kyats, but then I fixed it up. Flush toilet, kitchen, bathroom, the works—that came to eighty thousand. Now it's worth a lot more. Everyone in Taungbyon knows Madame Bond's two-story *nat* villa—oh, yes they do. It's a big deal.

Daisy Bond does things in style. Let me tell you, my processions aren't your common affairs. Processions are how we *natkadaws* pay tribute to the Brothers, carrying trays of bananas, coconuts, sweets, and other delicacies up the Grand Palace steps and dancing in their honor. It's the most important ceremony in a *natkadaw*'s life. You feel low and inferior until you have a procession under your knot, but once you do, you're inscribed in the official register of royal tributaries. After that, you can put up a sign saying you're a bona fide adept admitted to the court of two Taungbyon Brothers.

Processions as we know them didn't exist in the old days. *Natkadaws* just used to dance before the iron gates. But when the shrinekeepers saw them dancing with lots of money in their hands, they said, *Come on in. Don't dance out there. Come dance inside and make it official.* Now they're the ones who grant permission to go up and dance before the Brothers— for a price. It's become this whole craze.

In the old days, not too many *natkadaws* held processions. They weren't so expensive, you didn't have to pay any fees. All you needed were formal offerings of bananas and coconuts and extra treats for the *nats.* Maybe some palm wine—before the Brothers were observing sabbath vows, that is. What did it cost? Two or three hundred kyats at most. Me, I went out and spent a thousand. I bought apples and a huge cake specially

ordered from Yangon and those imported Golden Pack cookies. Not just anybody's sticky rice and fried fish or guavas and
pineapples. I ordered a tailor-made procession gown of the
best material and put on real jewelry, diamonds and gold I
borrowed from my relatives. And you know how I went up to
the Palace? I had bodyguards on either side just like Madonna.
Me and my two bodyguards up at the head of the procession,
and all the relatives trailing behind, that's how I did it.

Even now that a single procession runs upward of ten thousand kyats, I've never wanted for patrons. I'm good for a cool
three or four processions. Every year my relatives back me at
least one time; my *nat* sons and daughters bankroll the rest.

Some *natkadaws* are so eager to hold processions, they'll do
anything to find backers. *Amele!* They cook up such stories,
it's exhausting. How being a patron will help business and
make everything go right. This'll succeed, that'll come through,
you name it. We cook up crazy hopes 'cause we have to eat.
What *natkadaw* can afford to lay out ten thousand from her
own purse? There's the costume, offerings, and food trays, and
now you have to pay procession fees too. Plus you have to
give three big bolts of *longyi* fabric and six headscarves.

They say they're asking more than a thousand kyats for
procession fees this year. The *longyi* fabric will cost you another four or five thousand or more, depending on the quality. And nowadays you can add on as many snacks as you
like—these are imported-cookie times, right? One box will
set you back four or five hundred. And imported soft drinks;
the prettier the can, the higher the price. So a *natkadaw* has to
go chasing after patrons from festival to festival like a crazed

slut looking for a lay. Once we find ourselves a patron we can tell ourselves we're set for the year and feel that big ball of worries dissolve, but even now there's lots of *natkadaws* who've never done a procession. Deep down inside the desire's always there. We *natkadaws* all dream about processions.

Well, don't you worry about Daisy Bond in that department. The world is my lotus pond. You don't see me all bothered about processions or Ministers' turbans like everyone else. For me, the whole point of coming to Taungbyon was to have fun; becoming a *natkadaw* was a means, not an end. I ran around for two or three years trying to avoid palace people and their ministerial honors when every other *natkadaw* was practically panting, *Turban, turban!* I didn't want the responsibility. I just wanted to dance and sing and talk dirty, but they tracked me down and forced this turban on me. I guess I was too outrageous, this hot Bond Girl had them all fanning their scorched little fingers.

The truth is, I'm supposed to attend the Grand Council tonight. I'm a turbaned Minister after all, but if I don't feel like going, I won't. I already went and paid plenty of respect as soon as I got here to Taungbyon four days ago. Having to sit around in full formal dress with everyone, sweating and chafing, on and on until I can't take any more. Just thinking about it makes me want to scream. So it's decided, I won't go. If they want their damn turban back, fine. They can come and get it. I am *not* going.

"IS DAISY BOND in? Is she upstairs? Oh, Daisy Bo-ond?"

Oh, no, guests again. Just when I was about to take a little nap.

Daisy Bond sits up and rubs his eyes. He takes his glasses down from the shelf and puts them on, sips tea to rinse out his mouth, then wraps his *longyi* loosely about his waist in woman's fashion and shuffles out to the veranda to spit.

"Hello? Daisy Bond?"

"Oh, Ma Khin Aye. Come up, come up. When did you arrive? Did you bring my preserved shrimp?"

"Yes, of course. Should've arrived yesterday, but there were problems with the train tickets. We had to break our journey in Mandalay, then catch the nine o'clock train. Barely made it for today's Council. Ah, I can't even tell you how tired I am."

"You didn't get an upper-class ticket?"

"Yes, but no sleeping car," answers the wealthy patroness of a jewelry shop on Shwebontha Street down in Yangon. She bows respectfully three times to Daisy Bond's *nat* shrine, then pulls a five-hundred-kyat bank wad from her gold-clasped brown leather bag and hands it to Daisy Bond, who raises it to his forehead, closes his eyes, and starts to pray. The new bills exude perfume.

"Dear Buddha of unblemished, infinite power, infinite karma, and infinite wisdom, hear your Sunday-born daughter who holds precious the Triple Gem, Buddha, Dharma, and Sangha. O Guardians of the Faith, Lord Mahawathonderi who watches over this entire Earth; Lady Thuyethadi who stills the waters; Lady Sandiparami who commands the Seven Devas, Nine Devas, Ten Devas, and Twelve Devas; the eight thousand wizards; all the many teachers of teachers; Mercury Wizards, Iron Wizards, Potion Wizards, Numerology Wizards, Cryptogram Wizards, Charm Wizards, Incantation Wizards; the sixty-four

Sorcery and ninety-six Alchemy Masters, O Thirty-seven Nats and umbrella-honored hundred and eleven Regents, *nat* Kings and Queens most highest, maternal *nats,* paternal *nats,* grandmaternal *nats* and grand-paternal *nats* of this Sunday-born daughter, in keeping with the traditions of her father, mother, grandfather, and grandmother, yes my Lords, today she has donated for flowers and earrings and turbans.

"O Great Lord of Mandalay, O Taungbyon Bobogyi and Bobolei, your *nat* father Lord Mahagiri and the Seven House Spirits, this Sunday-born daughter spreads her hair at your feet. Smile on her as she bows, laugh as she kneels. Starting here and now, bring this one seller a thousand customers, promote her Tuesday-reigned diamond trade, her Wednesday gold trade, her Thursday emerald trade, let her Friday travels be safe and smooth. Vest her with amber, ruby, silver, and gold mines; keep her family together always without worry or querulous words or want, nor even a whisper of these things on the wind. Let her donate to the poor and feed the hungry and clothe the needy. Let her escape this secular world of attachments, let her do meritorious deeds for the Buddhist faith and clergy like King Thawkathiridama; give her power and glory to attain nirvana . . ."

The five-hundred-kyats' worth of recitation leaves Daisy dry in the mouth. Well, it's not just the money, it's loyalty and consideration. Ma Khin Aye is a good customer—that is, a dear *nat* friend. Someone he can trust.

They've known each other a good long time, so their friendship is strong. Daisy buys gold from her shop and when Ma Khin Aye needs a *natkadaw,* she calls on him. Daisy will

never change gold shops and Ma Khin Aye will never change
*natkadaws*.

Daisy finishes his tea, and still Ma Khin Aye's eyes are
closed, her lips murmuring. What more can she possibly want?

"Hey, anybody downstairs? Bring us up some tea and tea-
leaf salad."

At that, the wealthy jewelry shop owner opens her eyes and
bows three times.

"How's business, Ma Khin Aye? I recommended your shop
to one of my relatives who wanted to buy diamond earrings."

"Yes, she told me. She bought a pair."

"See? Kodawgyi and Kodawlei gave you money."

The wealthy widow lowers her voice to a whisper. "I want
more money. Pray for me."

"Oh, you rich people. You have money enough for one
life, but still you needle Kodawgyi and Kodawlei for more.
Must you be so greedy? Lord Buddha and the *nats* don't like
greedy people, you rich bitch!" Daisy's mouth is going like a
machine gun. "How about a boyfriend?"

"Oh, stop now! Please." Ma Khin Aye looks askance,
clearly bemused. "Must go now, but I'll send over the preserved shrimp."

"Fine, just come back in time for dinner this evening. By
the way, did your daughters come along with you?"

"No, I came with Daw Mya Mya from Kyaukgon and her
party. They say they'll drop by later to pay regards."

"*Amele!* Daw Mya Mya already has a *natkadaw*, that Moulmein Mi Ngwe. Why would she come to me?"

"Well, they *will* come. I already told them to."

"No, you didn't! I don't want to be stealing other *natkadaws'* disciples at my age. I don't need the money or the grief."

Protest as she might, Ma Khin Aye just smiles and heads downstairs. Daisy quickly tucks in his *longyi* and waddles after her. "Coming to my procession tomorrow evening? It's okay if you can't; all my relations will be there anyway."

"How many processions does this make for you this year?"

"Four. Care to make it five for the Quintuple Gem— Buddha, Dharma, Sangha, teachers, and parents?" It's an occupational hazard, this motor mouth. Wouldn't wheedle for a mere fifty or hundred kyats, but who'd pass up a thousand? The more processions, the more prestige.

"Only rich folk sponsor processions, my dear Daisy. You can't expect me to—"

"Go on, get out of here. Now. Before I start swearing." Daisy pushes her out of the gate. In the squalid huts across the way, other *natkadaws* look on enviously, but Daisy merely gazes down his nose at them, their thick makeup and bright red costumes, the way they roll cowrie dice and dance to attract customers.

"Spice that sauce! Stir it up! While you're young and juicy!" shouts Daisy, closing the gate behind him. Then turning toward the kitchen, he calls, "Ahpongyi, is dinner ready?"

The old *meinmasha* cook doesn't answer. Ahpongyi just stands there shaking an angry finger at someone. "Not so fast, you. It's not even five o'clock. I know what time you got in last night. There's work to do, guests to feed. I've only got two hands, you know. What am I supposed to do?"

"What is it, Ahpongyi? Tin Tin Myint again? What's going on?"

Sitting on a narrow wooden cot in the open area under the house, Tin Tin Myint wears a man's *longyi* breast-high like a woman and puckers at a hand mirror, putting on a few finishing touches of makeup. Ahpongyi is livid.

"Just look at her! The sun hasn't even set and the girl's raring to go out."

Ahpongyi's such a spinster, thinks Daisy, a real stick-in-the-mud. And not-so-sweet-sixteen Tin Tin Myint's the complete opposite. What a pair.

Tin Tin Myint was an outcast when Ahpongyi took the village youth on as a helper. The boy was dying to come to Taungbyon, so, like most young servants, Tin Tin Myint works all day for no pay, but has evenings free for dancing and cruising for partners.

"So hot to trot, you hardly cleaned the fish," scolds Ahpongyi. "They're still full of sand!"

"Calm down, Ahpongyi, let her go. I was like that when I was young. Maybe even worse. Nights, I never came back at all."

Tin Tin Myint breaks into a big smile and continues brushing on eye shadow.

"Better watch what you say, U Ba Si. Soon she'll be bringing all her tricks back here to the house." Ahpongyi always uses his old friend's real name.

Daisy leaves Ahpongyi to his grumbling and Tin Tin Myint to his primping. Only he can't go upstairs without adding a little taunt. "You know, Ahpongyi, I've been thinking, we should get you married. Hey, Tin Tin Myint, find Ahpongyi a man." Then suddenly Daisy stops halfway up the stairs. "Speaking of husbands, Min Min hasn't come back yet. If I don't miss my guess, he's with a girl. Hey, Ahpongyi. Min Min sure goes shopping a lot in Mandalay. What did he say before he left?"

"He said if it gets too late, he'd be back tomorrow morning," answers Ahpongyi.

Ahpongyi's cool words lodge burning hot in Daisy's chest. Uh-oh, he's going to stay in Mandalay. Is he seeing some girlfriend of his? He didn't tell me anything about sleeping over in Mandalay.

Madame James Bond is now in a fighting mood. Does he think he can get the better of me? If he doesn't come back, I'll go to Mandalay in the dead of night. And not to beg him to come back, either! Just to shake him down and get back my jewelry! I knew he was up to something, psyching up since morning to go out. He shot out of here faster than a caged bird, a horse from a stable. I just know he's seeing a girl. He's sick of this old fag. He's going to leave me for a real woman. Is that how it is? Go on, leave me! Why should I worry about a fucking husband at my age? Didn't I set him up in a good position? If he doesn't want it, fine. So go, good riddance. *Bing-bang-bong*, away, away!

Daisy pulls the hem of his *longyi* up high and rushes upstairs in a fit. He tries to open the wardrobe, but it's locked. The jewelry box is inside and *he* keeps all the keys. He takes care of everything. How kind of him!

Daisy plops down, deflated. If that's the way the little lover boy wants to do things, let him dare. I'm already gone on him, what can I do? What more can I give him?

See over there on the clothesline? Those three shirts we bought in Yangon just before coming to Taungbyon? Imported shirts he was so jumped up about, I had to shell out six hundred for each. Hmph, now the fucker isn't coming back . . . but then he wouldn't leave those shirts, would he?

Oh, *dokka, dokka.* I get these deep pains in my chest. A bitter pill I won't be able to swallow until he comes back.

That's the gay life: a life of laying low and putting up. Even as men, we're one step lower down. Whatever the man wants, we have to payroll and provide. It's our karma. Maybe I insulted someone's wife in the past, so now I'm half a woman in this life. We may be men in body, but we're really and truly women in our minds. We want to dress, eat, live, speak, sing, and think just like women. And yes, we also want husbands. Really, I can say this because I've been through it all. Don't even think about changing us. Try to convince us nicely or beat it out of us, it can't be done. Never. The *meinmasha* mark is on us from the moment we're born. We hide and mask it for different reasons, but come the right time and season, it blossoms bright and bold. Nobody can stop us. Nobody.

I know from experience. When I was a child, my family saw I was more like a girl and they tried to make me over. They put pants on me and bought me a toy gun, when I really wanted to wear a skirt and play house. They couldn't persuade me, so they beat me. If I painted my face with *thanakha*, they spanked me. If I tucked my *longyi* to one side like a girl, they hit me. But did I change? No, your son is gay.

Then when I came of age, they tried to arrange a marriage for this eligible bachelor. Me, with a girl? Well, with my fair skin and nice face, some women *do* fancy me. Somebody ought to tell them. Ha, one hometown gal's still waiting for me, poor dear. I can't help it if I'm not interested in women. As soon as I was born, this baby was grabbing the doctor's hand. Eventually my parents gave up on me and let me get on as I liked.

Going around Yangon with friends, we'd run into older sisters who taught us a thing or two about life. And heartbreak. Beginners get their hearts broken all the time. My first few falls were bad, but now after so many scars, my heart's shored up.

Maybe it's just too painful to think how all my young boys have ended up ditching me. I'm so giving, and they want the shirt off my back. Most boys I've had, when the time comes, they find a real woman and leave. All I know is, they want fresh catch, not smelly old squid. Oh, at first they prattle so charmingly, always staying so close, melting my heart so I'll give them whatever they want. I let them take me for everything—my blood, my body, the *nat* money I keep in the turban, everything. But then a month or two on, they start acting funny. More and more they're off somewhere fishing, which leaves me on the hook again.

How's Min Min any different? So far so good, but now after seven years, he's stepping out with his rod. Can't prove anything, but when he disappears the whole day for no reason and comes back any time of the night he damn well pleases, or sometimes says he's not coming home at all, I know something's up.

Still, I've managed to hold on to him for seven overpro-
tecting, overreacting years. He and I are such different ages,
what am I supposed to do? If I want to love him, I will. If I
want to punish him, I will. Even beat him if I have to. Min
Min is mine to do with as I please. I *bought* him for five hundred kyats.

I met the little bastard upcountry seven years ago. He was
sixteen and I was forty-six, the age when beauty blossoms, so
naturally he liked me. I was dancing in a *nat* ceremony and he
was in the crowd watching me. Later he told me I was just so
beautiful in my Lady Popa dress. Don't even ask if he was my
type. A good-looking boy like him, fair skin, tall with a good
build, big round eyes, those eyebrows of his. Even the way he
combed his hair. Only one thing put me off—he was dirt
poor. One look at his rags and you knew it. Well, I took pity
on him.

So I'm dancing and thinking, *There's a precious ruby in the
rough. If I wash him off and let his true colors show, I'd have myself
a movie star.*

Later that evening, after changing out of my costume to go
down and bathe, I see the boy again. The lady who hosted the
ceremony is working him hard. Him and a grown woman
and a little girl. Again I feel pangs of pity.

But as luck would have it, the lady has the boy draw water
for me. Ooh, I couldn't wait another second. I was already in
love. This Bond Girl makes up her mind on the spot. I walk
right over to the well and ask straight out, "Listen, how'd you
like to stay with me?"

No answer. He just gives me a nervous laugh.

"No, I really mean it," I tell him. "Would you like to come along with me? I'll take good care of you. You'd work for me and accompany me wherever I dance in *nat* ceremonies." I'm laying it on thick, but all he says is, "I'll go ask my mother."

Well, I beat him to it. I was so happy, I practically skipped over to his mother, that woman he was working with. The little girl was one of his boatload of siblings. So I say, "Your son here wants to come along with me, how about it?"

But then she just smiles, so I insist, "No, this is for real. I'll feed your son very well, see he has good clothes. Just say the word and I'll take him."

She hesitates, then it's "I don't know. It's up to him."

Finally the lady of the house breaks in and says, "Listen, Daisy, you want him for keeps? You have to buy him from his mother." Half teasing but half serious.

Well, you don't have to tell Daisy Bond twice. "Done," I say. I shoot upstairs, grab five hundred kyats, run back down, and push it into his mother's hands. "Here. From now on, I own your son, okay?" She nods and breaks into a big smile at the money.

From that moment on, I *own* Min Min. He's my servant, in charge of preparing my *nat* ceremony outfits top to bottom, then afterward he tidies up, takes the flowers from my hair, puts away my jewelry for safekeeping. But most important, whenever I'm possessed, he's the one who wipes my sweaty brow, oh so tenderly. Eventually he became my lover.

I watched him carefully for three years. Never once let down my guard, though he wasn't particularly smart. In the end, he won my complete trust with his simple honesty in handling my schedule and finances and messages. I depended on him for everything. I'm no statue. I'm flesh and blood like everyone else.

Yes, I became attached to him. I entrusted my entire life to him. I let him do as he liked, however he wanted to arrange things. I left everything up to him.

Let me tell you, the human mind is a scary thing. As soon as I gave him a free hand to run things, he changed completely. He started shouting at me and went missing for days, only to tell me he had things to take care of. Past public transport hours, he'd sleep over—wherever. And all the time, I'd be beside myself, not eating, not sleeping, just hoping he'd return.

Calm down, Bond Girl, calm down. Just lie on the mat, head on your pillow, relax. Even if you don't feel like eating. In the old days, wherever I sent him on errands, I'd say, *Come back in time for dinner so we can eat together.* He'd come back by mealtime exactly as told. Or if I felt tense, *Massage my neck . . .* Oh, stop now. I shouldn't be thinking about him. All this pain and anger wears me out.

"U Ba Si, shall I serve dinner? I already made the preserved shrimp salad," Ahpongyi shouts up from the bottom of the stairs. "Your light's not on. Are you going to sleep already? I thought you wanted to eat. Should I bring it up to you?"

"No, not just yet. I want to concentrate on my prayers. So don't let people up, Ahpongyi, you hear me?" Daisy slips a rosary on his wrist, then goes out to the veranda overlooking the street and yells, "Hey, turn on the light. Do I have to sit in the dark?"

Ahpongyi's heard it all before. He just shakes his head and flicks the switch.

"Say, Ahpongyi, did Min Min have many things to buy?"

"Many? I don't know. Tomorrow's your procession. He said he had to get you orchids."

"*Amele!* So he uses orchid hunting as an excuse for sleeping over! I just knew it."

"He might not sleep over. The buses run until nine or ten, so there's plenty of time to make it back."

"Oh sure, for anyone who *wants* to."

Ahpongyi refuses to pursue this discussion any further and slinks back downstairs. Daisy sits cross-legged on a mat and says his rosary while watching the people below.

Oh, these terrible burning flames. They consume you at sixteen, now here I am still flaming at sixty. Can't concentrate on my devotions. Damn you, Min, you give me such pain. If you don't want to come back, fine. I'll just pray you're happy. I won't sic the *nats* on you or spite you with curses. The day you stop loving me, just *go*. What can *I* do about it? Take all my jewelry, I can live with that. You'll get what you deserve. I'm not one to obsess over material things. The *nats* will keep me fed. Go ahead, spend the *nats'* money, if you dare. You and your wife and children and all your relatives, spend it, I dare you! Yes, my Lords, all I have I owe to you and the other *nats*. I've never hoarded or hid anything from you. If you feel like punishing him, go ahead. Teach him a lesson.

Daisy slips the rosary back onto his wrist, looks toward the Grand Palace and prays, then goes back to telling his beads.

What time can it be? It's getting late and the bastard's not back. Is it just this one night or forever?

Calm down, Bond Girl, calm down. Daisy stretches out on the mat, head on the rattan pillow.

Now I don't feel like eating. Used to be when I said, *I want to eat together,* no matter where he went or what he had to do, he'd be back on the dot.

Daisy rattles off a prayer and tries to sleep. *O my Lord Buddha. O Buddha, Dharma, Sangha. My calves are stiff from sitting all day and cooking up talk to make money for him. Must I reap the karma of all my past misdeeds?*

Used to be if I said, *My back hurts,* he was only too happy to massage me. Enough, don't think about the bastard. Though if he doesn't come back, it'll look bad. The girls will talk, *Daisy Bond's boy up and left her. He couldn't even wait for her procession. Took her things, too.* Well, let them talk. Just don't let me hear or I'll swear a streak, I will.

All the prayers, aches, and pains weigh heavy on Daisy's eyes until he dozes off.

*Min Min, Min Min.* It's him. Someone's calling his name. Is he back? Daisy rises with noticeable effort. It's him, he's back. He'd know that voice anywhere.

"U Ba Si, U Ba Si, you asleep?" asks Ahpongyi. "Min Min's back."

"Yes, I know," answers Daisy, trying to disguise the turmoil in his own voice. Daisy hears steps on the stairs. He rubs his eyes and comes in from the veranda to find Min Min at the door lugging two bulging shopping baskets. "Hey! Do you have any idea what time it is?"

Min Min is clearly upset. He drops the baskets on the floor with a thump and lifts a sling bag from his shoulder. "It's only eight o'clock. There was so much on the list, it took forever. I practically had to kill to get orchids. You stay home and gripe, you have no idea!"

"Well, if you can't get orchids, make do with some other flower. Didn't I tell you to substitute for things you can't find, didn't I?"

"Sure, you always *say* that, but you're a big name. You need orchids for your hair on your big procession day. I found spider orchids for your yellow *longyi*, but I had to go all the way to the orchid farm to find purple and white orchids to go with your purple *longyi* and the red dance outfit."

Daisy squints. Oh, how I want to hate him, choosing my costume for me! Can't I wear what I like? Not that I'm complaining. Yell at me, boss me around, he *is* the man of the house by now. See how different he looks these days? A changed creature! Imported *longyi* from India; blue-striped sport shirt; wristwatch; one-karat gold necklace, ring, and bracelet. Handsome, I must say—and not just because he's my pet.

"What's this? You didn't put away the turban money again. You leave it out in plain view? Just put it any old place and see what happens."

"Hey, nothing's missing. I'm up here the whole time. Who's gonna come and take it?"

"Yeah, you're here all right. You're here on the veranda sleeping. You wouldn't know if they marched in and carted away the works."

Tell me about it, Mr. Know-it-all. Mr. Can-do. You say

I'm sleeping out on the veranda? Hmph, I'm not sleeping at all. I'm on the lookout for you. So I don't put donations away. Let them steal it all.

"You really have no idea. I came as fast as I could, but the car broke down on the way back. I'm starving. Have you eaten yet?"

Daisy eyes him tenderly. An orchestra is playing dance tunes in his heart, but true to form, he can't just shut up and let things slide.

"You really didn't eat anywhere?"

"Oh, c'mon. Where would I have to eat?"

"How should I know? You might have somebody to eat with. You swear you haven't eaten yet?"

"Don't talk stupid nonsense when I'm hungry. I'm not swearing anything."

There he goes. Whatever I say, he gets all angry and impatient. "Well, are you going to wash up? Go on."

Min Min trudges off in a huff to take a shower. He's so cute when he's mad, makes a girl want to just slap him on the butt.

"Hey, Ahpongyi, where's the food?" shouts Daisy.

Ahpongyi brings up the preserved shrimp salad, but no sooner does Daisy Bond dip up a spoonful than he feels even hungrier than before.

Just a moment ago, I thought I was full. There's the human mind for you, the mind. Here I am, over fifty, and still these things get to me.

**4**

# BATHING
# DAY

*Now we live so far apart*
*How I miss my old sweetheart*
*Whisper winds, where does he stray?*
*The little boy who used to play*
*In our distant village*
*Before we came of age . . .*

A lilting voice floats in and out of the noise this fourth festival day. Wending down alleyways, past rows of huts, a sweet melody that enchants all who hear.

*. . . Padauk blossoms in full veil*
*Canopied the hills and trail . . .*

The voice makes its way through the teeming crowds to Daisy Bond's gate, but grows weary and pauses just outside. The yard is alive with guests for Daisy's procession this evening, a full house of *nat* lovers upstairs and down, an unending queue of guests to be fed. They crowd around Daisy, his red cosmetic case and its expensive contents spread out on a wooden cot while a niece helps him put on false eyelashes.

"Did you get to see the ceremony this morning? In all that pushing and shoving?" asks Daisy, lifting his face for the finishing touches to his immaculately blushed makeup. "No one pickpocketed you, I hope."

"I could hardly see a thing. The Palace was swarming like a beehive."

"Didn't I tell you? Bathing Day crowds are impossible . . . Hey, this side isn't even. Do it over again and glue it on good. Be a damn shame if the bugger drops off," he bitches, checking his lashes in the mirror. "Believe me, it was even worse in the old days. Back then, the ceremony wasn't at the Palace. They did it on a raft in the river. Carried the two Lords by litter down to the raft. Such a ruckus you never saw! People left and right reaching out to touch them, offering flowers and money. The litter could hardly inch forward, the bearers had to whip everybody with canes just to clear the way. *Amele!* What beasts! They could hit you, kill you, anything to clear the way, no blame whatsoever. Someone had to keep hold of the statues or they'd get knocked off, the crowds were so bad. But down at the river, the ceremony was a sight to behold, especially when the water was nice and high like now. They'd moor the raft at the water's edge and just slide the

Brothers on, then everybody followed in their boats. Otherwise they'd have to traipse through the mud and wade out to the raft before rowing over to the islands. Villagers from all over would paddle out to offer towels and *longyis* and loincloths for bathing. Even now that they don't bathe the Brothers in the river anymore, old-timers still bring those same offerings to the Palace. From last night, you see lots of villagers there from all the different local traditions: boatwrights who lash together bamboo rafts, oarsmen, rope pullers . . . They come here to Taungbyon every year. Even if they move away, they never forsake their vows. So remember, never forget your creed—or your man's seed, that's what I always say!"

As usual, Daisy Bond finds any opportunity to break off polite conversation and change the subject to sex. Especially among the ladies.

> *. . . How I miss those idle hours*
> *When the padauk was in flower . . .*

The pining voice arouses such sweet melancholy, Daisy's guests open the gate and invite the music makers in.

"What's all that?" asks an aunt as Daisy brushes on blue eye shadow.

"Just beggars, singing for money. There's so many of them here."

Crouching at the gate is a pudgy teenager with a ratty old *longyi* for a shawl and a cloth-covered earthen jar for a drum. Next to her, a boy who can't be more than ten holds plastic bags of food scraps in one hand and a small pail to collect money in the other. Beside him, the owner of the enchanting voice proves to be a mere wisp of a girl, perhaps sixteen or seventeen, her face half hidden beneath a towel.

> *. . . Not a moment I regret*
> *Nor a hair can I forget*
> *Searching ever as I might*
> *True as day must follow night*
> *In monsoon rain and heat and chill*
> *My feet now wander where they will . . .*

The chubby girl drums on her jar while the singer rings finger cymbals and snaps clappers in time with either hand. Everyone falls silent in awe of the sad, sweet voice.

> *. . . How long further must I journey*
> *Along this road of mystery?*
> *The seasons pass, I wander still*
> *Over valley and stream and hill*
> *Crazed with love, no peace I find*
> *He's forever on my mind . . .*

Her violinlike tones bewitch one and all, including Min Min, who stands quietly by the washroom door preparing purple orchids for Daisy's coiffure. Suddenly he sees Daisy waddle out, only half made-up and *longyi* loosely knotted, determined to ruin the lovely mood with that squawking of his. Min Min scurries after.

> *. . . In every secret dwelling place*
> *Wherever love may hide its face*
> *I search out my long-lost friend*
> *Forever searching with no end*
> *Crazed with love, I find no rest*
> *An arrow pierces through my chest.*

The chiming stops, the voice vanishes. The pail on the ground fills with five- and ten-kyat notes.

"Hey, girl, your voice isn't half bad. What about your looks? Let's see your face."

"Please, Daisy, no-o!" But before Min Min can stop him, Daisy pulls away the towel.

Min Min will never forget the moment. Who could forget that charming face, so pure and innocent? A beauty mark peers out from between two coal-black brows; her eyes swim with pathos.

"Why cover up with a towel? You're pretty enough. What's your name?"

"Pan Nyo."

*Pan Nyo.* Min Min repeats the name to himself, but Daisy interrupts.

"That's justicia, the *nats'* flower. Who named you? Were you born here at the festival?"

"No, nothing like that."

What does Daisy think he's doing? Can't he see he's scaring the girl?

"Why beg like this? Wouldn't you rather sing in the *anyeint?*" Daisy turns to one of his followers and says, "Hey,

Mr. Producer, what about the girl? Think you can use her as a singer? She'd make a good actress. I'll give her a dance costume. How about it?"

Daisy's theater-owner friend smiles, but Pan Nyo shrinks nervously, moving to leave.

"No, stay. Sing!" Everyone in the yard pleads with the girl.

"You all eaten lunch yet?" Min Min hears himself ask. "Guess not, eh? Better eat a little something, then sing."

The lovely eyes steal a glance at Min Min, then are gone. Quietly, just above a whisper, she answers, "We'll eat with our grandmother. She's waiting for us at the wayside rest house."

"C'mon, have a little something. It's almost two o'clock."

"No, we're fine."

"Hey, Min Min, feed them!" shouts Daisy Bond, returning to his makeup.

You bet I will. I'll give her plenty of food. Beans like for all the guests and fried chicken, too. I'll even throw in some of Daisy's cassia soup. It's supposed to be good for those who use their voice. You can't always be eating other people's leftovers, Pan Nyo. You should take care of the gift Lord Buddha gave you.

> *All them jade miners say*
> *Gonna get rich someday*
> *I'll strike a big gem*
> *Be wealthy like them . . .*

Min Min whistles along while packing their food. Hmm, he thinks, she can do up-tempo numbers too. That's some range, from laments to bouncy tunes, a voice to bewitch people.

> *. . . But when their plans fail*
> *They sit and sell nails*
> *The rice may be gone*
> *Still gotta keep on*
> *If this hole don't hit*
> *Go dig one more pit*
> *And if that one don't pan*
> *Dig a thousand again . . .*

More and more small bills drop in the begging pail. Min Min folds two forty-five-kyat notes and tosses them in quickly so Daisy won't see. He can just hear the squawk, *How can you waste my money? That's my* natkadaw *earnings!* Flying his tatty old *longyi* battle flag. Not a pleasant prospect.

"Here, li'l brother, rice and curry. Careful now, or you'll spill the soup."

The boy accepts one of the plastic bags Min Min hands him, then the three of them walk out the gate.

Min Min follows them to close the gate, and whispers, "And just for you, Pan Nyo. Cassia soup, so you won't lose your voice, okay?"

The towel-covered head nods—or maybe it just bobs forward, Min Min can't be sure. She doesn't turn around.

"Mi-i-in Min! Oh, Master Min Min!"

Uh-oh, here he comes. Shouting right on cue. The ol' fag's a hard taskmaster. Doesn't cut me a moment's slack.

"What? Why?" answers Min Min, heading under the eaves to where Daisy is just crayoning on his lipstick and closing the cap.

"What d'you mean *why?* Bring me my costume. And my jewelry. Where are the flowers? Where's my turban?"

"Everything's laid out. It's still early."

"Oh, is that so? Look at the clock! What's the time?"

"Almost three o'clock."

"You call that early? We have to be ready and waiting at the Palace steps by four. Unbelievable! *Go!* Get everything down here. *Snap, snap!*"

Min Min hears the ladies laughing as he turns to go upstairs. Min Min can just see Daisy smirking like a wife who'd never slight her husband to his face but sneers behind his back. She does that act better than a real woman.

Purple silk classical dance *longyi,* cream-colored silk blouse, purple turban, purple orchids, white socks, and gold-embroidered sequined slippers. . . . Min Min places everything beside Daisy Bond, who beams with satisfaction.

While Min Min opens the jewelry box, Daisy wraps and unwraps his turban five times this way and that—sheer nonsense for such an experienced *natkadaw.*

"Stop, let me do that for you. You'll never make the procession at this rate."

All smiles and poses, Daisy tilts his head up ever so accommodatingly. The picture of smug triumph, he pretends to not even care that his young lover has just wound the turban over his eyebrows like a bandage. But not a moment later, when Min Min steps out and the women distract themselves, he quickly readjusts it. He's wrapped these things a thousand times in his *natkadaw* career. How could he not know how? He just wanted proper attention, that's all.

"Here's your pearls. If you go with the amethyst pendant, you'll want to drape a long pearl necklace on top. And a braided gold chain, too, okay?"

Delighted at Min Min's thoroughness, Daisy gives him a meaningful *Anything-you-say-dear* look.

"Min, the flowers for my coif!"

Min Min pins on the flowers and helps Daisy into his dance costume while the women giggle at his antics.

"Hey, ladies, pull yourselves together. How're we doing for time? We should be going. What's my number?"

"Twelve, number twelve. There's still a way to go. Someone just went and asked, and they're still on procession number eight."

"Good, good. All the offerings ready? Banana trays, *longyis*, snacks?"

"That's *my* job," scolds Min Min. "Your job is to keep still."

"I will *not* shut up . . ."

The ladies cheer Daisy Bond's snappy comeback. Now he'll really act up and start foul-mouthing. Min Min just smiles and gets on with his job. After so many years, this is nothing. At sixteen, the company of women and their ribaldry were strange to him; he wanted to run away. But by now he's an adept, he lives with it.

"Number nine's on! Number ten's up next!" squeals young Tin Tin Myint, messenger boy for the day. His urgent progress report from the gate sends a wave of excitement through the whole house.

Resplendent in royal purple as U Min Kyaw, Lord Governor of Pakan, Daisy Bond starts out first. After him come the principal donor couple, each with banana-and-coconut trays, followed by their retinue carrying fruit, cakes, imported cookies, *longyi,* scarf and turban fabrics on gold lacquer stands, and polished steel salvers. All are dressed in their best clothes and jewelry, the better to raise their *natkadaw's* stock.

"Everyone take off your sandals and leave them here," Min Min reminds them before leaving. They don't want to be losing their expensive footwear. There's no place to store sandals at the Grand Palace and nobody to watch them, nor should anyone cross the sanctuary in front of the two Lords holding filth from their feet.

They head out. People all along the path to the Palace gaze in admiration. Novice *natkadaws* rolling cowrie dice in their thatch huts, barely able to cover expenses for this one Taungbyon pilgrimage, look on enviously at the grand procession.

Daisy Bond and company arrive just as group nine is leaving by the main doors and group eleven is queueing up at the steps, waiting for the side doors to open. Which means group ten is already inside before the Brothers. The shrinekeepers guard the gates assiduously, checking each person, letting no one in but verified participants.

As group eleven enters and the shutter-doors accordion shut again, their group moves up to the foot of the steps. Daisy raises hands and bows to the nearby huts where senior *natkadaw* Queens and Ministers stay. These VIP rooms around the Grand Palace aren't free; they go for two thousand kyats each, but the good location gets more game. When aged Queens retire from Palace duty, they tell fortunes and do dice readings. The Ministers, too. What else would they do for money?

"Woo, Mommy, you look so be-eautiful!"

Uh-oh, who's that? It's Sein Ma Ma from Moulmein. My, my, isn't *she* all glittered up. "You, too, honey. You look just like, uh—what's her name? That movie star, Something-Something-Bo. Hey, somebody help me."

That's our Daisy Bond. One of his followers shouts out— *Htun Aeindra Bo!*

"Right, you look like *her*, Sein Ma Ma. So you're number thirteen, are you?"

"That's right, Mommy," says Sein Ma Ma, hands clasped respectfully at his breast.

Daisy's right, Sein Ma Ma is made up to look like the popular actress. He even imitates Htun Aeindra Bo's laugh, her enigmatic smile, her proud delivery. Whereas Daisy Bond prefers male roles like U Min Kyaw. Each *natkadaw* to his specialty.

It used to be that female spirit dancing cost less, but now the fees are the same. You had to offer more snacks to please female *nats*—Lady Ngwe Taung, for instance, demanded separate servings of sticky rice and fried fish—but then they gave you more time to dance, at the least an hour and a half. Not anymore, though. With so many *natkadaws* on the scene now, lords and ladies both get the same fifteen minutes.

Well, well, Sein Ma Ma's got herself lots of supporters, all dressed to the hilt. She's really come up in the world. Must be hitting forty. A couple more years and she'll be in peak form. To parade up with such numbers at this early hour is quite an achievement.

The processions start at three in the afternoon. Any spirit wife who gets a turn by eight or nine at night is a real VIP *natkadaw.* Those past midnight with numbers in the seventies and eighties don't rate. Nobody knows their names. The only ones who come look at them at daybreak are peddlers hawking beans for breakfast.

"Pretending to be a tiger, are we? Miss Macho Daisy!"

"Ooh, don't you wish! You slut from Pyi."

The *natkadaws* of different groups greet each other with taunts and teases, back and forth, sizing up the others' outfits and accessories while waiting their turn—sassy fun and games only true initiates know. It's a high, a thrill that makes all the wheedling and coaxing customers the whole year round worthwhile.

"The tens are almost finished," Min Min calls out.

Daisy strains his ears to hear . . . yes, U Min Kyaw's pounding theme music. Group ten is almost done. They'll be let in any second now.

"Everybody, please. Check your neighbor. Don't let anybody in who's not part of our group. Make double sure."

Min Min handles these duties very well. He's a leader. He takes up position beside the shrinekeepers to personally pass as many processioners as he wishes. Otherwise, the guards might arbitrarily limit their numbers.

"Come on, come on. Everyone this way."

The tens exit. Now the folding grille doors pull back, and at Min Min's rush call, the group quickly files inside.

"Hey, you, over there. Who's that butting in? Beat it."

Min Min spies someone trying to sneak in with them and sends the stranger scurrying. Always a concern for shrine-keepers and participants alike. With so many people parading through and money changing hands, tight security is of the utmost. Robberies at the Palace are not unknown.

Immediately, women from the Palace staff begin checking all the offerings. Do they have the requisite number of ba-nanas and coconuts on their trays to propitiate the next *nat*? Did they bring enough fruits and snacks and sweets? Three bolts of *longyi* fabric? Material for six turbans? On down the production line, transferring each item to the Palace's own waiting ceremonial vessels in presentable order. It's one pro-cession after another in here, no time for people to fuss about reclaiming their property afterward. That's why the Palace provides its own containers and someone from the *natkadaw*'s house has to mind their wares, making sure they're not set down somewhere and lost in all the activity. There's no one here to take responsibility for any of that.

One fat staff woman sits on the tile floor groaning about her aches and pains. Even working in shifts, they're never equal to the massive task. No shortage of hands, but they don't ac-cept outsiders. Only relatives of the shrinekeepers are granted Palace duty.

"Quick now, if you want your picture taken with Daisy Bond," Min Min tells everyone. Contracted photographers flash away inside the main hall. Outside cameras are not allowed into the sanctuary; they have Palace exclusives. Videos are also available for a price, to be settled up when paying the procession fees.

Daisy Bond and company have only taken four or five snaps before group eleven's trance music winds down.

"Let's go, let's go! Offering trays on heads! Pick up those snack boxes! Everyone single file. You, head of the queue, quit dawdling! What're you waiting for?"

Min Min rushes about getting everyone ready. Though nominally in male attire for her role today, Daisy twinkles coquettishly to see the boy marshal such command.

"Number eleven's done. Get in, get in, hurry up!"

Min Min leads everyone inside. By the time they're in position in the main hall, there's not a trace of the previous group's offerings. All the bananas and coconuts and snacks have been carted off to a back room. Daisy hurries up to the enshrined Brothers even as the elevens are still on the front steps. A drum signals it's time to start the ceremony. There's no time to waste, not with so many processions still waiting in the wings.

First, Daisy bows to the two Lords and the Queen Mothers seated in a row out in front, then kowtows to the Seven House Spirits. The orchestra skips the customary lead-in and launches straight into the cockfight theme for U Min Kyaw, the drunken gambler spirit.

*U Min Kyaw from golden Pakan rides his horse and calls—hey, hey, hey!*

Daisy Bond prances and sways holding up a brass donation bowl. As he swirls the bowl high and low, the principal donor steps up and puts in three thousand kyats. The others follow with lesser "bets," then take their places on either side of the "cockpit." No one but the Queen Mothers, Ministers, shrinekeepers, *natkadaw*, and followers are allowed inside the iron-barred enclosure. No one except for two policemen standing guard.

Over against a barred door sit the musicians. From three o'clock when the processions start, that door stays locked. Spectators must watch from outside and content themselves to pass any flower offerings through the bars.

*U Min Kyaw from Pakan the Golden rides his horse and calls, calls, calls! . . .*

The singer watches the "bets" amass in the bowl and cleverly keeps "calling." He obviously recognizes U Ba Si, a Minister, the kind of big name to make big money, otherwise he'd only chant one "call."

*. . . Come on, come on, come one and all!*

Over and over again the come-ons repeat. Three times Daisy mimes U Min Kyaw drinking and gambling. Swigging from an empty bottle, a shabby paper rooster tucked under one arm, he cavorts incorrigibly to up the "ante." The first two rounds he presents decorously to the Brothers. The Palace takes a minimum of four thousand kyats or two bowls of two thousand each, though with the donor's three thousand and the others' contributions, they're well over the mark.

One of the staff women busily stuffs the bills into a white rice sack that is filled to bulging—and this is still only procession number twelve. By dawn tomorrow, after all the processions are done, they'll have five or six huge bags full. Which explains the iron bars and police guards.

*. . . Come on, come on, ol' Papa Kyaw calls!*

Daisy flings the last bowlful at the musicians, then continues shaking and gyrating, fanning five hundred kyats' "finale money" in either hand.

*. . . The Palace calls, go, go, go!*

The musicians eye the cash and play lively, their shouts echoing like a roaring tiger. Daisy especially loves that. He'll give away any amount of money just for that roar, that rush. Here's for you, musicians! And for you, guards! Daisy tosses up the last few bills, a flurry for all. Let them fly between the bars to any takers outside!

It's a play for keeps, Palace take all. The *natkadaw* only comes away with his costume and a bit of glory. Fame but no fortune, though some *natkadaws* do try to stash away the last handfuls of dancing money in their *longyis* when no one's looking. Even Daisy did it when he was young, but in this day and age there's no hiding. Last year they nabbed a young *natkadaw* whose light fingers showed up in a video replay. What a scandal!

"All right, time to leave. This way, everybody!" shouts Min Min as the music stops.

How many minutes did he dance? More than the allotted fifteen? Daisy always gets a few extra minutes for the "face" his money buys. Poor late-night *natkadaws* who can't pay the musicians may only get nine or ten minutes of dancing, but that's the breaks.

Min Min exits and waits on the steps for Daisy and the others to emerge.

"U Ba Si, U Ba Si! Get yourself over here!" barks Min

Min. He always uses Daisy's real name when he's angry. Daisy gives him a nasty look, then wraps a big hank of his classical *longyi* around his neck to safeguard his jewelry before venturing out into the crowds. Still, he has to admit, Min Min is a good bodyguard. To and from these sessions, he never leaves Daisy's side. He's so conscientious, so attentive.

Turning the corner back toward the house, Daisy unwraps the *longyi* yardage from around his neck and begins to channel a voice. "Papa's drunk, *urp!*"

It's U Min Kyaw after a wild night out. The drunken spirit loves him so much, it tags along like a butterfly. Now begins Daisy Bond's favorite after-session routine.

"Hey, somebody, roll out a carpet on the cot," shouts Min Min as soon as they get home. Daisy sweats like crazy after dancing, it's best he rest awhile under the tamarind tree. Min Min turns to Daisy's U Min Kyaw and bids, "Face forward, m'Lord. Up here, m'Lord."

"Yo, offer me drink!"

Min Min brings out a bottle of soda and a straw while the donor lady fans Daisy.

"Ho, court lady there. Your Lord's gonna do the rounds of the other palaces. Wanna have a little fun with Papa?"

"Yea, Lord, I shall follow."

Daisy Bond hops down off the cot, holding the pop bottle aloft.

"Yo, daughters and sons, your Lord's gonna make merry at my Shan Cousins' Palace. Coming along?"

"Yea, Lord, we shall follow," all present intone, palms pressed together in respect.

"After that we'll visit ol' Six-Arm Shiva, then Papa's own Palace!"

They all cheer and applaud. Papa Daisy belches and leans on Min Min. "Come, young princeling, keep me company." The older he gets, the more all this dancing and what-not wears him down.

*Nat* music blares from hundreds of little shrine huts, each with its own band and minor *natkadaw* processions. Young *natkadaws* who can't afford the Grand Palace do their processions at these "lesser palaces" for four or five thousand kyats. You don't have to offer three bolts of *longyi* fabric. All you need is booze and fried chicken and snacks. The fees run around five hundred kyats—nothing compared to the Grand Palace—though you still have to lay out fifteen hundred for the "cockfight" and "finale." The lesser shrinekeepers hold sole authority and get to keep everything. One good thing, though, they give you lots of time. Each *natkadaw* gets a good two hours to dance.

Even after a Grand Palace session, some groups like to make the rounds of the "lesser palaces" just for the hell of it. To Min Min's way of thinking, it's a bit like those street spectacles during the Buddhist New Year Water Festival, where famous singers go around performing their hits on different local stages, only here it's famous *natkadaws* putting in guest appearances at different shrines. They all love it with a passion; it's such a thrill. They get to act up with a full complement of followers in tow, U Min Kyaw's wild butterfly flitting from this shrine to the next.

Min Min also enjoys these lesser shrines, it's nonstop carefree fun from one place to another. All the processioners like it, men and women. The energy, the physical release, the freedom—it's an open invitation to party in honor of the successful completion of their Grand Palace procession. Min Min gets to drink at all these "lesser palaces," as do all the men in the group.

Just look, everyone's so beautiful under the colorful lights at the Shan Brother and Sister's Palace. They're all getting loose, happy to leave their troubles behind.

> *Come on, come on, comin' through!*
> *Been feeling bored now, haven't you?*
> *So let's all go out and sing a few*
> *At the Taungbyon Brothers' fair!*
> *We'll tease and joke and laugh and swear*
> *Don't get mad, it's the custom here!*

This *nat* music gets into your system and puts you in high spirits—then, oh, how it tickles the love blood. So when Min Min finds himself pressed up against a girl at the shrine, both of them intoxicated, what's to stop them? Who in this crowd of *nat* lovers could blame anyone at a time like this? Far from it; many fall in love. Min Min knows only too well, and even knows from experience.

Over there, one of the group tries to stuff a ninety-kyat "gift" down a singer's blouse, but she just accepts the man's blurry admiration and deftly tucks the money away without dropping her smile. And there, a girl and a drummer in the band make eyes at each other across the flushed audience.

And here a *natkadaw* in full female spirit dress waiting his turn to dance after Daisy kindly catches some young prospect just about to keel over.

> Gold smile, silver smile
> Taungbyon freestyle
> Making whoopie, having fun
> Come upcountry, everyone!

Someone tosses up a storm of small bills. Ones and fives shower down all over the shrine. People push and shove, hands straying as they reach for the new bills. Min Min grabs a five-kyat note that just happens to be in a girl's hand and then keeps holding on. Our drunken procession patron chases a one-kyat note to where it lands on a lady's breast, but the woman just laughs him off.

The whole time Daisy poses and prances, he keeps one eye on Min Min, making sure he doesn't get out of line. But Min Min ignores him and keeps on partying.

Oh, let me *be* for once. So what if I enjoy the touch of real female skin? The pleasure that arises when male and female come in contact, it's a law of nature, isn't it? People can't go against their nature forever. But no, big bad Granny Bond will never understand.

"That's it, Papa better be going. If I hang around this shrine any longer, I can see this spirit's going to get his butterfly stolen."

Everyone in the audience laughs but Min Min. He hurries out of the shrine with a nervous frown. How can he face that girl who was so generous with her hand? Daisy Bond is forever upstaging his forays, warbling *That's my man! My love!* to Min Min's constant embarrassment. As if there were anything he could do about it.

*From dawn to dusk till moon comes out*
*You wander 'round the town and shout*
*Toting palm wine, rum, and beer*
*You better mind the neighbors, dear*
*Drunk by day, drunk at night*
*It isn't proper, it's just not right*
*I can't go out and show my face*
*Pakan Kyaw, my sweet disgrace . . .*

Daisy and group now reach their last stop, U Min Kyaw's own Pakan Shrine, where they're greeted by this year's latest song. The shrine hut is packed with boys of all ages who share their patron saint's taste for liquor, jumping, and swaying in abandon. The shrinekeeper extends an effusive welcome to the great turban-wearing Palace Minister Daisy Bond and makes space for his followers. The bandleader also bows hello from his circle of drums.

*. . . Hey go, go, go!*

Just now a *natkadaw* is finishing his dance, doling out fistfuls of finale cash. He hands a forty-five-kyat bill to veteran *natkadaw* Daisy as etiquette prescribes, then bows and leaves. The bandleader spontaneously grabs the microphone and dashes off an intro to the ever-popular, drunken, butterfly-possessed gambler spirit.

"Silence, please! The grand and glorious Lord Mayor of

Pakan, U Min Kyaw, whose attributes are legendary through-
out the land high and low, hastens this way. Sound the royal
drum!" A buffalo-skin tom-tom sounds—*boom!* "Presenting
that father figure to us all, who drinks on special occasions,
whose drinking *is* a special occasion, U Min Kyaw!"

"*Urp!*" Daisy Bond gives a signature belch, attesting to
Papa Kyaw's spiritual presence. Everyone in the shrine roars
with approval. Now a songstress with bright red lipstick steps
up to the microphone.

> *I'm so tired of telling you*
> *Every little don't and do*
> *You refuse to understand*
> *The duties of a good husband . . .*

She camps it up, wagging a shrewish forefinger at Papa Kyaw
while Daisy's followers cheer with glee. One appreciative fan
staggers over to give the singer a little "token."

> *. . . When the sun starts to descend*
> *You're out drinking with your friends*
> *Sunup, sundown, 'round the clock*
> *You'll be betting on your cock . . .*

She lays on the nagging prude even thicker—and reaps even
more tips.

> *. . . Pillar of virtue, you saint of the street*
> *Without you around, no party's complete*

*Why for once can't you be nice?*
*Listen, Kyaw, a word of advice:*
*Maybe try drinking a little bit less*
*No more gambling, no mistress . . .*

As the music builds to a frenzy, bandleader Sein Paw Lwin bounces to the beat.

Gotta play like a demon, Papa Kyaw's cockfight's coming up. The *natkadaw*'s little fuckbuddy's already passing around the bowl to cover his bets. He'll clear a thousand kyats for sure. I been playing drums at this shrine for twenty years, I can tell who's good for a thousand kyats and who only a hundred.

I *have* to know. Can't *not* know. That bowl's my life. The more money in the bowl, the easier I breathe. The more money in the bowl, the better I play. Three cockfight rounds, three bowls of money just for me. Let the shrine owner and shrinekeepers have those last handfuls of finale cash, ol' Sein Paw Lwin cleans up on "cockfight bets," "blade-honing fees," and "boat-caulking charges." *Natkadaws* shouldn't figure into it. Aside from U Min Kyaw's cockfights, it takes money to sharpen Lady Shwe Gaing's knife, Shan Sister Palé and Brother Myo's swords. And the Taungbyon Brothers need their cere-monial boat fixed up regularly, right? Those fees ought to come to us musicians, but the *natkadaws* and them all want their cuts. It's not fair. They already get their procession fees and dancing cash and banana-tray whatever. They should leave some for us. We don't play for free, y'know. Gotta pay the shrine owner and shrinekeepers, too. I have to give this Pakan Shrine five hundred to show my gratitude. Plus one thousand more to cover utilities for the seven days of the festival. It's these seven days when ol' Sein Paw Lwin's orchestra gotta make money from every *natkadaw* who comes here to dance—whatever it takes to fill a bet bowl or shine a sword or patch a boat.

The money's okay. This is U Min Kyaw's own shrine after all. No shortage of processions, the stream of *natkadaws* isn't drying up. And if things do get quiet, Papa Kyaw always brings in some of his drinking mates. The money comes, but I still got my expenses. With a big group, there's meals and such to think about before I clear any profit. Three thousand five hundred to truck our kit each way up and back, plus three to four thousand for food. So altogether, that's more than ten thousand up front.

Didn't cost nothing in the old days. Wasn't but one band to play for the whole village. Not so many *nat* shrines neither, not all over the place like this. Only a few originals, the Seven House Spirits' Shrine, Royal Clerk's Shrine, the Wizard of Mandalay's Shrine, Ma Me U's Shrine, Mother Se Daw's Shrine, and that was it. Later on, a few more like Talaing Kyaw's Shrine, this here U Min Kyaw's Shrine. Then there was the Shan Brother and Sister, the Pyi Kan Daw Brother and Sister, Mother Yé Yin, Ko Thein Shin, Shwe Nabé, Bago Nan Kayaing, the Pathi Brother and Sister, Tha Paik Mé Daw, Ma Ngwe Taung, Hpo Nyo, Thaik Nan Shin, Man-isithu, the Danin Wizard, Ywadaw Shin, Kamé Pyin Bobo, Ko Myo Shin, Palé Yin . . . who can keep track of 'em all? Year after year, the whole damn country's shrines are gathering here in Taungbyon.

Why all the increase in shrines? Well, it's pretty clear to me. As this Taungbyon Festival gained popularity nationwide, everybody's getting into the act, cashing in on the *nat* cult to make a living. So many people wanting to become *natkadaws,* especially gays, and with no real *nat* calling, either. They take injections for their charm, those *natkadaws,* so they can swish and sing and dance so sweetly.

Savvy *natkadaws* want their own shrines. They buy out property in Taungbyon at twice the value, build their own shrines, and put up some *nat* name or other, and become shrine owners. Then there are shrine renters who work out some deal so they can divide the take. Here at this shrine, fr'instance, the money from the first festival day goes to the shrinekeeper. After the full moon, each time we play everything goes to the shrine owner. In between, the share you get depends on the deal you cut.

Ever since the festival took off, lots of musician wannabes come this way too. That was the start of this damn pay-to-play system! Everyone checks which shrine rakes in more than the others and they fight to put down their money. Wasn't much at first, nothing like we pay today. Back when U Tin Aung was the bandleader here, he paid just one hundred kyats for five days, 'cause he only had to play after Bathing Day. In the old days, folks wouldn't dare play till the two Lords returned from the river. We even sent messengers to the Palace to be sure, but nowadays it's not like that. At first light on Bathing Morning, the whole village was banging away.

All us groups got to bickering so much, we formed the Nat Orchestra Brotherhood. This was back when the Young

Monks' Charitable Association was in charge of the festival. In upper Burma alone, Mandalay music groups was competing among themselves, and as if that wasn't enough, bands from Yangon was coming up to Taungbyon too. So us NOBs protested to the YMCA and they sent all the Yangon groups packing. Ever since then, no Yangon groups can play here and the orchestra fees have stayed fixed at five hundred per festival year.

It ain't easy, ain't easy at all. The fighting for popular shrines still goes on. The more powerful the shrine, the more money it makes, the more they fight over it. Different shrines got different powers. Some shrines got human power, some got *nat* power. Shrines patronized by the swank with rank, where the big-name professional *natkadaws* go to dance, are human-power shrines. Needless to say, human-power shrines make more money. But this Pakan Shrine where I play got both human power and *nat* power. Seems to me, Papa Kyaw's spirit don't want to let me go to no other shrine; he just keeps me near him.

People ask me, *Sein Paw Lwin, you make your living playing* nat *music, do you believe in* nats? Well, of course I do. Ol' Sein Paw Lwin believes in *nats*. Didn't even used to have my own band, but after playing at this shrine here, I done bought me a place instead of renting. If I didn't believe in *nats,* who would? Listen, when the August 1988 protests shook the whole country, all the musicians in Taungbyon went running back to Mandalay to pawn their gold rings and jewelry and bells and gongs, but I walked away with maybe five thousand. No problems here. I been playing U Min Kyaw's shrine for twenty years and never once have I gone home empty-handed. Last year, I got over thirty thousand kyats, more than I ever got before. Usually it's more like fifteen or twenty. So sure, I give thanks to U Min Kyaw and the two Brothers each and every night, I do. They support me; I can feel it.

Whoa, speaking of support, look at all the dough that fell into my lap from the betting bowl. Yes indeedy, lots of two-hundreds. Better bow nice and respectful when I hand back the bowl.

"Hey, who gave you this orchestra? Eh?"

"You did, m'Lord. Papa Kyaw done give me all I have."

"So, bandleader, whose disciple are you?"

"Papa Kyaw's disciple, m'Lord. A very dear disciple, m'Lord."

"Right, and Papa Kyaw's gonna give you more, much more. It's Sein Paw Lwin and Papa Kyaw, just us two, just us two. So let's *go!*"

"Hey! *Go, go, go, go!*"

Sein Paw Lwin's huge hands beat the circle of drums relentlessly. As always, Daisy Bond lays a forty-five-kyat bill on top of each drum, and Sein Paw Lwin, his face dotted with beads of sweat, shines a bright smile.

Give us more, Papa, give us more. Enough for the transport truck. And ward off any competition; don't let us stray from this shrine.

Somebody peels out a bank wad, and new one-kyat notes rain down all over. Sein Paw Lwin knows this *natkadaw* very well. He's generous, but then he can afford to be. Got a fine flock of followers, got donors for five or six processions a year.

Some *natkadaws* can't swing no donors. No class. They
don't talk the talk, ain't got the stuff. Imagine, coming here
and only bring us one measly two-hundred-kyat bowl. Some
come in and dance, then leave us musicians twenty-five kyats.
Times like that time, I grab the mike and let 'em have it. *Listen, you* natkadaw *punk. Don't think you can pull that one on me!
Like I'm just so glad to drum and sweat away while you dance? I
want money, got it? I want a fair price for the music we play. What're
we supposed to do with your twenty-five kyats? C'mon, out with it.
Lay three hundred kyats on these drums and not a pya less. You're
not setting one foot outside this shrine till you give us that money,
punk. Just try it, I'll learn you not to mess with Sein Paw Lwin, I
will.* The things I have to do.

I swear, please don't let me meet up with cheap *natkadaws*
like that ever again. Please always send me *natkadaws* like this
one who spend money like water. Five or six *natkadaws* like
Daisy Bond a day and I'll have money to spare.

Daisy flashes Sein Paw Lwin an "okay" hand sign—*Enough
for now*—and the bandleader brings the music to a sudden
stop. Daisy bows, then droops into Min Min's waiting arms.
The old girl's just very tired or drunk or who knows what.
He might drink and dance like a man when possessed by Papa
Kyaw, but soon as the spirit goes, he's snuggling against his
young man's shoulder.

"Min Min."

"What?"

"I'm drunk, I drank too much."

"Fine, you can have a nice sleep at home."

"Mm, sure. I'll sleep with my head on your chest."

Min Min goes quiet. A bit of the silent treatment, as expected, then a little scolding. Nice and soft, *What a hassle you are, woman.*

"Min, darling, did you hear me?"

See? I call him darling, like when it's just the two of us, and not a peep. Darling Min, don't you love me anymore? Are you tired of me? No matter how cool you get, I'm still in love with you. We're going to sleep heart to heart tonight.

# 5

# PALACE PROCESSIONAL

THIS BUSIEST DAY OF THE FESTIVAL, WAVE UPON wave of bodies swelter under the hot sun. Music blares all over. Everywhere you hear chanting, *Go, go, go!* Today the cowrie dice rumble like tremors. The tiny huts are full of people kneeling attentively, consulting *natkadaws,* each swaying in trances of different spirits. Most often they're possessed by the two Lords or by U Min Kyaw. It's Papa Kyaw in this hut and Papa Kyaw in that hut, the Brothers Shwepyingyi and Shwepyinlei in this hut, the Brothers in that hut too. All who consult the Taungbyon Brothers and Papa Kyaw, bowing in respect and sitting with legs to one side, come to ask for a "lift" of one kind or another.

"Lift" me, O Lord, to succeed in business. "Lift" me in the sweepstakes. "Lift" me with a winning lottery number. "Lift" me with a promotion. "Lift" me out of here to go abroad.

"Lift" me so I can build a real brick building. "Lift" me so I can buy an XE Sedan. "Lift" my sons and daughters to pass their medical school entrance exams with honors.

The two Lords and Papa Kyaw are only too happy to pronounce, *Wish granted!*, and demand shows of gratitude in return. Papa Kyaw's spirit will always ask, *If Papa gives you that "lift," what'll you do for him?* Barter, if you like. *When it comes true, my Lord, I'll offer you gambling money and processions aplenty.*

Today, nameless *natkadaws* roll out white sheets at the Wish-Fulfilling Pagoda, set down money bowls in front of them, and talk in tongues, but they only get ten- and five- and one-kyat bills, not nineties and two-hundreds like at the shrines. Dirt-poor villagers drag in from all around to consult these *natkadaws,* staying overnight in the pagoda compound on five-kyat mats, lighting makeshift cookfires in the morning. There are touts at the pagoda compound who rent out mats and very cheap food stalls, and just outside there's something of a little vegetable market.

Today the mat dealers and ready-made banana-and-coconut-offering-basket peddlers and bright-scarf merchants are all happy. There are stalls selling *paisang* seeds, like the ones the two Brothers used to play with as children in their human existence. People buy those big dry discs to offer at the *nats'* own skittle pitch, so the shopkeepers are happy too. The flower sellers are in bliss; they can sell offering bouquets with their eyes closed. All the tradesmen are happy—hawkers vending seasonal pineapples from up north in Myitkyina or cold drinks and special festival snacks or Taungbyon souvenirs and trinkets, even pickpockets—everyone who depends on the waves of pilgrims is doing just fine.

People walk around with glutinous rice steamed in banana-leaf parcels, sweet rice-flour pancakes, and sticky rice bars with palm sugar and coconut shreds, and sport garish fake gold necklaces and bracelets—all pushing and shoving toward huts where their two Lords and Papa Kyaw keep manifesting. But at the big house near the Grand Palace, the *nat* who possesses our Daisy Bond is neither Brother nor Papa, but the "Crude Mama" Amé Gyan whom womenfolk especially enjoy.

"This Mama's from the street, ha! That's why I'm so rough and my mouth's so dirty. Mama likes her drink. Mama's husband, Ko Tet Ka, was a famous thief. Rather than get robbed, the king knighted him Royal Treasurer. He had it good, the lout. He didn't come back to me, so Mama followed him to the capital! I saw the Royal Guard out marching, but what the hell's a country cunt like me know? The king said, *Who dares cross in front of me?* The soldiers came and grabbed me, but I was so drunk on palm wine, I swore a fucking streak at the lot of them."

All the women titter at Amé Gyan's obscenities. Ordinarily they wouldn't deign to listen, but a channeled *nat* is a different story. Daisy puffs on a huge corn-husk cheroot like a tough old bird, nibbles at tea-leaf salad, washes it down with swigs of alcohol, and talks as dirty as he likes as his showmanship gains momentum.

"So, then they said, *Where does a common village girl get off being so rude!* And they struck me dead on the spot. Wanna hear just *where* they beat me?"

"That's enough, Mama, we don't need the details," cautions Min Min, well acquainted with Daisy's love of smut, but Daisy just shoots Min Min a sharp look.

"Who the— *Amele!* Is that you, Ko Tet Ka? My darling?"

Talk about embarrassing. Speak up, try to keep him under control, and it only makes things worse. Min Min is clearly not amused at having to prop up this Amé Gyan who's falling over him. How many times has he told Daisy not to act like this in front of people? Still he dare not blow his cool or walk away. Do that and Mama Bond can get a lot cruder than any Crude Mama. Min Min has seen it all before.

Once someone was sponsoring a ceremony for Amé Gyan and Min Min forgot to prepare a balsam-tinctured handkerchief like he was supposed to. So when Amé Gyan got to talking about her life and pining for Ko Tet Ka, a real tear-jerker routine, no matter how many times Min Min "wiped away the tears," no tears came. Only when Daisy leaned close to ask about the balm did Min Min realize he forgot. *Forgot?* Amé Gyan spit out such a streak of obscenities, he thought he'd never hear the end of it. How long did it take Min Min to live that one down?

"What you girls laughing at, huh? Ko Tet Ka is Mama Gyan's man! So hey, let's see some money for my palm wine and tea-leaf salad."

The women inch up on their knees to offer money while Daisy mimes a jittery Amé Gyan spirit with all her quirks, shaking his head and shading his eyes with one hand like an old woman straining to see.

"Hey, you. You swore a *nat* oath for the success of your

business, didn't ya? Mama's gonna make it happen. Good as done."

The lady bows and listens respectfully as Daisy continues foul-mouthing.

"Hey, you back there, all strung out about your brute. Come up here by Mama. Don't worry, Mama's gonna make him come back. With just a flash of Mama's skirt. Mama knows all about these things from when Ko Tet Ka left me. You hear me?"

A distraught-looking lady in gold and diamonds comes forward to offer a forty-five-kyat bill. Daisy rips the money out of her hand and tosses it away.

"Whatcha expect me to do with that fucking pittance? You can't cheat Mama. You didn't mind spending a bundle on black-magic wizard shit, hmph!"

"It's not like that, Mama, please forgive me. When Mama's son, my husband, returns home, I'll give you a ceremony."

"I don't want that. You want something done now, you do it now. You give hot air, then air's all you get. We *nats* get straight to the point."

Uh-oh, he's talking like Daisy Bond now.

Min Min, ever the middleman, looks up from fanning his master and smiles obligingly at the woman, trying to contain the situation. The lady opens her handbag and proffers a two-hundred-kyat bill.

"Curt like dirt I am. Crude's my name. If you're not feeling charitable, I ain't gonna rob you. If you're not satisfied, take your money back."

Look, look. He's doing it again. That's Daisy Bond's voice.

"No, Mama, they're satisfied. Next please!" Min Min quickly intercedes, signaling another lady and her problems. It's always the same with Daisy. He never listens. Their job is to wheedle money from people with words. His delivery has to be cool and clever. He himself even said, *I have to twist things nice and sweet*—but does he?

Min Min never thinks they twist the truth for a living. They simply squeeze those with too much money so that everyone gets a share. All the people who depend on *natkadaws* like Daisy Bond, from musicians and their families on down the line to coconut-and-banana sellers, everybody's got to eat. In these terrible times, at least this business can feed lots of households. Begging from people who have money to spare, what's not fair about that? Madame Hassle's wheedling supports so many. There's merit in that, good karma.

"Yes, yes, you'll get what you seek. Happy? Won't take hardly a wave of Mama's skirt, my daughter. See?"

Suddenly a group of women come barging upstairs just as Daisy's trance is hitting its stride.

"U Ba Si, U Ba Si, they made off with a necklace!"

"They did *what*—?"

Amé Gyan stumbles. The women calling Daisy by his real name are rich relations from lower Burma, this evening's procession donors.

"Whose necklace?"

Amé Gyan vanishes. Her spirit butterfly flutters away.

"My two-ounce gold necklace. Do something, U Ba Si. Ask your *nats*."

"Oh, c'mon, what can *nats* do about pickpockets? Didn't I warn you time and again? Hey, Min Min!"

He's shouting again. Shouting at Min Min for every little thing. And here he was, trying to keep this Amé Gyan crowd in their good graces.

"What's it now? What's with you?"

"What's with *me*? We have to file a police complaint. You go to the police station, I'm going to Ngwe Khin."

"Ngwe Khin? What for?"

"You know what for! People who get in a fix go to Ngwe Khin. She's faster than the police. Go, go! Do what I say! Got money? Here, take money for the police."

Look at him. He's reaching for the altar, about to grab that two-hundred-kyat offering from just a moment ago. But luckily the woman whose necklace was stolen saves the day by handing Min Min two hundred kyats.

Daisy adjusts his *longyi,* shuffles to the door, and steps into wooden clogs.

"Shall one of us come along?"

"No, don't need anybody else," shouts Daisy Bond, then storms off. Once out walking, he takes a pair of glasses out of his blouse pocket and puts them on.

I may be going on sixty and my eyes are getting dim, but at least I don't look over fifty. But now, where to find Ngwe Khin? If I have to search every single one of these huts, I'll die. That little faggot doesn't stay put. Here this year, over there the next, moving wherever she feels like. Vagrant trash, but the tramp's got a reputation.

Ngwe Khin is a fixer. Any mix-up or mess, he's the one

they all run to. Even so, he's forever broke. Money never stays in his hands for long, so the sisters all tease that he's Miss Moneypenny to Daisy's James Bond.

During the festival, anyone who wants to borrow at interest; pawn or sell gold, *nat* statues, cockfighting bowls, *longyi* fabric or dance costumes; trade husbands; or track down a thief, Ngwe Khin's the girl. He'll solve things faster than the police. Even pickpockets rely on Ngwe Khin.

Daisy Bond and him are old friends. Both are the same age, but Ngwe Khin came to Taungbyon earlier. By the time Daisy Bond arrived, Ngwe Khin was already wise to the whole scene. They met each other "iron gate dancing," and he became Daisy's mentor in all things shady. They danced the *nat* festivals down south together. Back then, they both had hair down to here. In lower Burma, people like their *natkadaws* with long coifs.

"Where to, Daisy? Lose your man?"

A high, nasal voice issues from a nearby hut, and Daisy returns the standard *meinmasha* greeting: "What's it to you, fatherfucker?"

It's Limp Wrist Mi Ngwe, holding a lit cigarette, all made up with flowers in his hair, sitting at a footed tray, tossing fortunes for some customer.

"Hey, Limp, where's Ngwe Khin keeping herself?"

"She's a *nat* fairy, she lives in Tavatimsa heaven."

"Just fucking tell me, where the hell is she?"

"I really don't know. Go ask someone else."

Daisy curses and storms off again. Limp never changes, even if she *is* starting to show her wrinkles. In their young gay days, Daisy Bond, Moneypenny, and Limp Wrist were an inseparable Taungbyon trio. All they knew was dolling up to go dancing and having a wild time. They'd stay out until the crack of dawn, then crawl back home to sleep, only to wake up, bathe, eat, dress up, and go out again. What crazy, happy days those were!

The three of them rented a *nat* hut together. A lot of people wanted to rent that year, so a greedy landlady named Thein Thein struck a deal with the local Buddhist monk to let out space for a *nat* hut on the monastery grounds for the three of them, seeing as they were "so very close." Didn't cost much, but just as they were moving in, the monk and Thein Thein got in a horrendous drag-out fight over the money and the three gays had to pull them apart. Whereupon the monk threw away their belongings and kicked them all out. They lost the roof over their heads, but had themselves a good laugh over their predicament.

"You'll see in the end, mark my words, Lord and Master Papa U Min Kyaw has good things aplenty in store for you!"

Daisy would know that over-the-top delivery anywhere. That can only be Nat Sprite Sein Claire, who just broke up with his man.

"The spirit butterfly lady's yearning for her squeeze. She just needs a good lay!"

Daisy shouts a taunt and walks away. Sein Claire must be fuming, but is too busy channeling U Min Kyaw to curse Daisy back.

Passing a tea shop steeped in blaring cassette music and rancid oil, a table of delinquents razz him, but Daisy just hooks them a pleased glance and a sway of the hips, glad to know he can still get a rise out of young boys.

"Where we headed, Daisy?"

It's Ma Lwan, that half-Chinese from Yangon. A university graduate no less, he wears glasses and keeps his slim figure and fair skin. Always cool and calm, he's a known name with many followers, but in typical gay *natkadaw* fashion he wastes all his money on his ingrate boyfriend.

This time Daisy Bond returns a civil greeting. "Ah, Ma Lwan. I'm looking for Ngwe Khin. Know where she's at this year?"

"Over where Highlife Hill used to be, is what I heard. You know the place, don't you? Just a little further north."

"Sure thing. Catch you later, Ma Lwan."

That damn Ngwe Khin will never leave Highlife Hill. The glory has long burnt out, but he still hovers around the ashes. Like Ma Lwan said, "used to be" big-city society wives from Yangon, Mandalay, Moulmein, and Bassein would gather there. The money flowed, the place was a free-for-all. All the *mein-mashas,* Daisy included, had a fine time plying their iffy trades. Oh, the tales of *natkadaw* husbands on the sly and rich bitches on the make, the stories of foxy faux-gays and horny heiresses. But sooner or later the money ran out, as did all the gold and jewelry—everything. People called the place a "high-living hell," and after a while it became Highlife Hill.

Back in its heyday, Moneypenny Ngwe Khin was the guru of Highlife Hill. Ladies who wanted to trade toy boys or sell bracelets and necklaces or buy birth-control pills and injections, they'd go see Ngwe Khin and he'd make the arrangements.

Ngwe Khin could fix anything. He was in the money. But by
the end of the era, those slumming socialites slid way down-
hill. Still obsessing over some Taungbyon loverboy, coming
back year after year to spend every last pya on him, divorced
without family or fortune, they had to scrape by cooking and
cleaning for the boy's *natkadaw* wife. Unbelievable, but hey,
that's karma.

Getting closer, yes, that whole scene used to be around
here. All the huts were decked out with outlandish carpets,
fancy four-tier tiffin carriers and huge ice chests, lace pillows
and satin cushions. Diamonds and gold twinkling top to bottom. Pets of every shape and size falling all over them, eating,
laughing, flirting . . .

Daisy Bond has his own checkered memories of Highlife
Hill. What was it brought him here last—or rather *who*? None
other than his own houseboy. One year, after waiting and
waiting for Min Min, Daisy finally got wind that he was here.
So the Bond Girl stayed up until four in the morning, prime
time for surprise scare tactics. Gave him the whole night to
prepare fighting words, script out nasty barbs to rip any protest
to shreds. Then he laid siege to the huts and started yelling at
the top of his lungs. "Hey, Min Min, get your puny prick out
here now!" Every filthy epithet he could think of—it was
sheer poetry. The whole of Highlife Hill went dead quiet. He
raised such a stink, vented such venom upon the whole rotten
heap, he practically shut it down then and there! Daisy re-
members dragging Min Min all the way home, waking everyone shouting, "See this shameless fucker!" Put the slam on
him big-time, gave the ball buster something to think about.

Daisy crosses toward some ramshackle huts, probably those very same ones, though nothing like they used to be. And predictably, in the last one on the corner, he spies the former superfemme changing his blouse.

"So the crone of Taungbyon is back, gray hair and all! Gonna reopen Highlife Hill?"

Recognizing Daisy's voice, the old queen sasses back, snipe for snipe. "Takes a tramp to know one. Us *meinmashas* all sell ourselves; *you* should know."

"True enough. We're whores, always have been, always will be. But you're the whore of all free-fucking whores." Daisy spatters more insults. Don't mess with Daisy Bond, this is one real *meinmasha* here. Never test our kind. As soon as we're born, out comes the marquee. "Nearly killed myself trying to find you, Miss Leaf-to-the-Wind."

"What's up? Why come looking for me? Time to change husbands?" Ngwe Khin responds with a trump of his own.

Ngwe Khin has his own inimitable style: a loud, untucked short-sleeved shirt over his *longyi,* one hand holding a drink, the other hand a cigarette. Round face and sharp lips, eyes blinking, *What's it this time? What you need done today?*

"Just now, one of my relations got robbed of her gold necklace. Can you make inquiries?"

"What's that to me? Do I look like a police chief?"

"Oh, c'mon, you got pickpockets poking you up the butt."

"You must be thinking of somebody else. I don't want any cops here. I don't know riffraff, and I'm no ringleader, so don't give me any grief." Ngwe Khin likes to lay on the sarcasm. "You got your own contacts, why come to me? You're a hotshot Palace Minister, you know bigwigs and swells. I'm just a poor *natkadaw*, what can I do?"

"Cut the shit, girl, and give me a drink. You do have booze, don't you?"

"As a matter of fact, I don't. So get off my back."

"Don't lie to me. I see that carton of rum you got there."

Ngwe Khin turns and surveys his hut. "Okay, you see the carton. Big deal. It's not mine. It belongs to two Chinese brothers from Mandalay who left it with me to sell. Yesterday, I drank one bottle, so now I'm out two hundred twenty ky-ats. The carton of Pepsi is something the girl from the soft drink shop dropped off to sell. Just now, I had to go buy a ten-kyat shot of local rotgut. So don't blow things out of proportion. That red curtain behind the altar I borrowed from Saya Tint in Myitkyina, the two offering trays are from my adopted daughter in the village, and that string of one-kyat bills a disciple hung up there."

"Hey, no need to boast."

That only provokes Ngwe Khin. "I'm on a seesaw here, I live things as they come. I can barely buy four cups of rice at a time. I just got one measly charcoal stove. The other day I go to the market and buy three clay pots. Good pots were fifteen kyats, but warped ones were ten kyats, so I bargained them down to fifteen for two. Good water pots were twenty-five kyats and chipped ones fifteen, so I got one with a broken lip."

Daisy can't even think of a comeback, he's laughing so hard. No one holds a candle to this vagrant tramp. Not even Daisy can touch his phony hard-luck stories. Anytime he runs out of money, he'll pawn his cockfighting bowl. It's real silver, after all. Then when one disciple comes into money, he'll just ask her to go buy it back.

Ngwe Khin has a history; it's always one thing or another. One time he asked to borrow a female *nat* dancing costume. Daisy wanted him to look beautiful, so he lent him the real article. An old-fashioned yellow double-lace, hand-stitched with pearls. Nothing but the best. This was also during the Taungbyon Festival. The loan was for a day, but the next day it didn't come back; two days and still no costume. Then one day, Daisy's young gay errand boy came reporting, *Mommy, Mommy, last night at the* anyeint, *I saw Yupayon up onstage dancing in your skirt.* That did it! Daisy went straight to the theater and burst backstage, shouting, *Where's Yupayon? Where's my costume?* You better believe Yupayon was ashamed. But the funniest thing, that troublemaker Ngwe Khin was there too, cowering under a blanket on the dancer's bed when he heard Daisy's voice. Daisy raised such a commotion, Ngwe Khin burst up from the blanket and threw the costume at him— *Here, take your damn dress!*—then stormed out. As it turned out, old Moneypenny had rented out the skirt for twenty kyats a night. That's his brand of trouble.

"Hey, want to sell your early procession time slot? I got somebody who'll buy."

See? He's already looking for trouble.

"No, I'm not selling. I'm too old for that kind of nonsense. It might have been fun when I was young, but not anymore."

Ngwe Khin glares darts and beaks his lips. "You talk awful damn big."

No, I'm not talking big. I really don't need the aggravation. Like my Min says, at my age it's high time for me to act dignified. Sure, in the past, I sold my procession slots for the hell of it. I was young and foolish. When I got a low number, other *natkadaws* who wanted a better time slot would buy it. Never fetched much, only two bottles of booze and a hundred kyats. Probably sell it higher nowadays. Not that I couldn't if I wanted to. I'm good for four or five processions a year at Taungbyon, maybe even two processions a day and always good slots. Sometimes donors don't show and you can forfeit your position, but otherwise there's no excuse. The Palace might not give you an early position again next year. Still, some people push things.

"Hey, this coming March, I'm going with you to the Pakan Festival, hear me?"

"*Amele!* No, don't come. Please no. I beg Your Ladyship." Now Ngwe Khin's got him scared. "And rent that boat again? What was it you said? The boatman's little mustache was so cute? Tell me again."

That was some trip with Ngwe Khin to U Min Kyaw's festival at Pakan. Like Taungbyon, all the *natkadaws* go there, though it's kind of a rough trip. You take the train from Yangon up to Mandalay, then a bus to Myingyan, then an hour by oxcart to the Irrawaddy and ferry across to Pakan. By the time we reached the river, everyone was so tired, we assigned Ngwe Khin the duties. *Go get us a boat, girl.* But what he hired wasn't a ferry boat, it was just a little putt-putt outboard motor job. No roof, no sides, no toilet. We were broiling under the sun and had to hold our bowels and bladders the whole way across. We all gave him shit. As it turned out, he didn't even bother to check the boat; he just looked at a notice board and took a fancy to a photo of the boatman with a mustache. What a character! Still, Ngwe Khin is reliable for some things.

Later in Pakan, they shared a two-story house with other festival-goers, and fought constantly over this and that—tea water dripping through the floorboards, Daisy's heavy footsteps upstairs, everything. Daisy got so angry, he threatened them, "I'll teach you, I'm going to tell the *nats.*" Whereupon he tapped Ngwe Khin on the arm and said, "Take care of this and I'll give you a hundred kyats." The next day, the women downstairs discovered all their belongings were gone—skirts, sandals, food containers, everything. Those women were so scared, they all up and left. Ngwe Khin was swimming in spoils. He bought himself drink and smokes and had money for his little friends. When Daisy Bond teased him, "Well, you could've at least left me one food container," he just said, "I didn't do anything. It was your *nat* aura." Though he still asked for the hundred kyats.

"So, Ngwe Khin, since you won't give me a drink or act civil, I'm out of here. Just listen up: The stolen necklace was an old-fashioned two-karat gold braid."

"Hey, I told you, I don't know a thing. Go to the police."

"Fuck you. You swear you don't know who did it, may the *nats* strike you dead?"

"Dead as said."

"May the *nats* snare you?"

"Snared as sweared."

"That's all. Do your stuff and come see me this evening. I've got guests at home and a procession this evening and I haven't done a thing yet." Impulsive as always, Daisy jumps to his feet and puts on his wooden clogs.

"Hey, give us some money."

Knew it. Just like the sleazebag. Daisy gives him a knowing look. "What money?"

Ngwe Khin's lips draw tight, her eyes brew. "They get you to dance for the *nats* and shake your fucking ass for free now, do they?"

Daisy laughs and slaps his empty breast pocket. "Don't have a single pya on me right now. Just come this evening, okay? I'm gone."

Daisy walks off and leaving Ngwe Khin cursing to his back.

MIN MIN exits the police station and starts home. If Daisy's not there, Min Min has to be. Who else is going to keep the customers occupied? When Madame Hassle visits friends, he's gone for hours. They all just talk dirty and joke around. He just hopes the old girl returns on time for this evening's procession.

Ducking into a back alley to avoid the festival crowds, Min Min passes Hla Thuza Mae's place. He tries to hurry by, but sharp-eyed Hla Thuza Mae spots him. Daisy would have a fit—*I suppose your feet just carried you that way?*

"Hey, Min Min, come sit awhile, why don't you?"

"No, can't. Still got lots to do today, Mommy."

Hla Thuza Mae, artfully womanlike with padded breasts

and full red lips, pouts playfully. "Don't be so cold, my sweet. Just for a bit, I've got something to tell you."

Min Min can't politely refuse, so he walks over. *You went and sat down?*—he can just hear Daisy—*You shameless flirt!* Hla Thuza Mae rents three huts together, all tarted up with synthetic silk drapes and trimmings.

"Your eyes are wandering. I know you're looking for something. Have some Mandalay rum, the real thing. Try the fried chicken." Hla Thuza Mae leans in closer with a naughty look on his painted face. "Got even better chickens, for your friends, or maybe for you?"

"Where? Bet they're expensive, the prices you charge."

"Accusations, accusations." Hla Thuza Mae turns toward a *nat* image and bows. "If I'm not telling the truth, may the *nats* strike me dead. Let me show you, just a second." Hla Thuza Mae is about the same age as Daisy, but seems younger because he rises and moves so effortlessly. "Here, Min," he beckons from a silk-draped doorway.

Min Min gets up to have a look. There inside the dimly lit room, Min Min sees a young girl with sleepy eyes and smeared makeup and another girl fast asleep.

"Well, how about it? Just this much." Hla Thuza Mae raises one finger—one thousand kyats. Min Min winces, but the gay madam merely raises an eyebrow.

The lazing thousand-kyat girl gives him a quick, professional smile, then goes back to sleep, whereupon the other sleeping beauty suddenly stirs. She gives Min Min a strange feeling: She somehow resembles the singing girl he saw yesterday, her unadorned face looks so vulnerable, so at a loss.

Min Min turns to go, and Hla Thuza Mae follows. "Leaving so soon? What do you say?"

"I'll be back tonight. Got a procession first."

"See you, then. Bring a friend and I'll pay you a commission."

"Yeah."

Hla Thuza Mae is out of control. He's into every possible vice and cuts deals on the side. No wonder Daisy Bond detests him and never accepts him as an equal. But then, Min Min thinks most gay *natkadaws* at this festival are just as low.

As Min Min walks between the rows of huts, he sees an old-time woman *natkadaw* shaking a head of white hair and chewing betel. Her white silk scarf and plain brown skirt seem so modest and dignified. Min Min bows from a distance. He pities these old women *natkadaws*; they get so few followers these days, so few remain in Taungbyon. Gays are much better at pleasing people, they put on a better show. Times have changed: To be a *natkadaw* today is to be gay.

Min Min takes a shortcut he knows, but today every lane and alleyway is jammed. He has to wade through seas of people.

> *Childhood friends, Athet and Too*
> *So happy now we meet anew*
> *How happy now we meet anew . . .*

A sweet, clear song steals through the roaring tides. That's her, yes; it's Pan Nyo. Where is she? Min Min scans the *natkadaw* huts. The drumming is getting closer.

*. . . Childhood friends, Too and Athet*
*Do you recall how we first met?*
*Do you recall the day we met? . . .*

Min Min fights toward the music. Over there, it's Pan Nyo, towel on her humbled head. And to either side, that chubby girl with the shabby shawl drumming on her earthen jar and the little bag boy holding up a canister for handouts of rice and curry. Min Min digs two fifteen-kyat bills out of his pocket.

Suddenly, there comes an outcry—*Pickpocket! Pickpocket!* A crowd rushes at him. Alarmed, Min Min jumps up into a nearby hut. Then, once all the squeals and screams die down, he sees the little combo's predicament: The boy has spilled all their food on the ground and Pan Nyo lost her towel. Though so much the better to see the girl's face. The dab of *thanakha* on her cheek looks so cute. And yes, she's a smart one. She's holding the begging bowl with all their money tight to her chest.

"You're such an idiot!" the drummer girl scolds the boy, his eyes swimming in tears. "You gotta hold on good. We can't lose that much food!"

"I lost my towel, too," moans Pan Nyo. "Let's go."

In a flash, Min Min is standing right in front of her. Ashamed, she looks around in panic for her towel. She scares easily.

"Come, I'll get you more food."

The drummer girl and the little boy look at Min Min, but Pan Nyo averts her eyes.

"Remember me? Yesterday, I gave you chicken and soup at the house by the Palace."

"Yeah, the house where we got lots of money," shouts the drummer girl happily.

"That's right. C'mon, follow me."

"No, we better not," comes Pan Nyo's whisper. "Grandma's gonna go hungry."

"If you don't come along, how will we feed your grandma? All your food's gone."

"We'll manage, we'll buy her something. Let's go," Pan Nyo repeats, then claims the wrap from the drummer's shoulders to cover up. The other girl makes no sign of protest.

"In that case, here's some money. Go buy your grandmother some food." Min Min drops his fifteen-kyat bills in Pan Nyo's bowl.

"You want a song?" she pleads quietly.

Min Min feels sorry, but wants to tease her. "Sure, what song?"

"I don't know. Any request?"

"So you sing requests?"

"Name your song," says Pan Nyo, eyes challenging from under her impromptu headcloth.

"How about 'To Whom It May Concern'?"

"Of course."

"Don't test her, brother. She knows lots of songs." The drummer girl breaks in, but Pan Nyo merely demurs with a smile.

"Do I have to sing? We really ought to be going. Grandma's waiting."

"Okay, go. Sing next time. But tell me, Pan Nyo, where are you all staying?"

"At the big ruined rest house outside the village." She bows humbly and starts off.

Min Min knows the place very well. Poor pilgrims from all over the country stay there. "You ever come out at night?"

"No, I'm too tired. After eating I just fall right asleep."

Except when singing, she's such a fragile soul.

"You following us?" Pan Nyo glances back to ask Min Min, now walking behind them.

"No, I go home this way." Then, heading off down an alleyway, he adds, "Come by the house again tomorrow, okay?"

The girl glances back at Min Min, and he winks. Oh, Pan Nyo, your bashful expression makes my heart quake. *Skirt chaser!*—Daisy would lambaste him—*Running after any woman who comes along!* He'd never understand, never ease up even for a second. Pan Nyo, would you hate me if I decided to go see that girl I saw at Hla Thuza Mae's?

THE AUGUST MOON dapples the veranda in silver light. Min Min slowly massages Daisy, one recumbent calf at a time, gradually letting up as his breathing relaxes. All that prancing and dancing, two processions at the Grand Palace and a further foray to a lesser shrine this evening have laid Daisy flat. He's impossible when he's drunk and tired. He mocks and fusses, he nags, *Hug me hold me fan me massage me.* He refuses to let Ahpongyi or Tin Tin Myint massage him, complaining *Min Min's touch is better, only Min Min hits the spot.* He's a sixty-year-old child. Perverse and naughty, he still wants to dress up, still wants to dance and play, though his graying temples show even by moonlight. After seven years of living together, Min Min has grown to feel some affection for him as a mother or a big sister—but not as a wife.

After Daisy falls asleep, Min Min shuts the door and tiptoes downstairs. Ahpongyi is having a quiet time smoking a cheroot stub. Min Min gestures to him, then as soon as he steps outside, painted faces loom up through the yellow lightbulb haze, bodies dressed just like real women slink around looking for one-night stands. Slithering snakes, they can smell who's tasted meat. They see Min Min and hiss, *Hello there, honey.* They smack flying kisses, they bat their eyes. They grab at Min Min's arms and squeal, *Don't you love me anymore?* They do turns, posing bust and derriere, teasing, *Not pretty enough?* Their heavy panting and lip-licking pursue him all the way to Hla Thuza Mae's brothel.

"You should stick to their kind," hails Hla Thuza Mae. "Wouldn't cost you a thing, might even get a meal out of it." There's no one in the place. The silk-draped boudoir is still.

"What gives?"

"Sorry, Master Min," shrugs Hla Thuza Mae, then laughs. "All taken."

"Fine. I'm leaving."

"No, wait. Here, have a drink."

Min Min gulps it down, then Hla Thuza Mae hands him a glass of water and a lacquer dish with tea-leaf salad.

"Want another?"

"No, thanks, I drank a lot at the processions this evening."

"That was fake rum. Mine is real. Try it."

"No, really, I'm fine."

Min Min heads toward the night market through a riot of music from shrine huts on all sides. Brash, wild rhythms daze and disorient him, banging bells and gongs make his pulse pound. All the drink and noise and lights make his love blood boil.

Min Min's footsteps lead him out of the village, toward the rest house where Pan Nyo said they were staying. Is this love? She's probably his for the taking. Just a singing beggar girl, but he feels sorry for her. He's halfway there when he thinks to buy a quid of betel to chew to cover the alcohol on his breath.

The outskirts of the village are pitch-black. Far off in the dark, silhouettes are moving in faint patches of light. He smells curry and piss, hears quarreling and children crying. Min Min watches from the shadows as people eat by dim candles.

Pan Nyo, where are you, girl? That female shape huddled under a blanket, can that be her? She must be tired and sleeping after singing so many songs all day.

Out of nowhere, Min Min hears someone whistling. A young boy skipping along the path up ahead is playing toss with a snack packet. It's Pan Nyo's little brother.

"Hey, boy. Where you been?" Min Min calls out as he emerges from the shadows, startling the boy.

"Oh, it's you, brother."

"Yeah, I came to visit you guys. Where's Pan Nyo and everyone? Are they sleeping?"

"Sister Pan Nyo isn't asleep yet. She sent me out to buy a pack of dried fruit."

"She likes dried fruit?"

"You bet. She always eats some before bedtime."

Min Min accompanies the boy to the rest house. All the poor people have staked out their own little spaces on the creaky, rotting floor. They all have their reasons for coming to Taungbyon; they all have to scratch out a living. At one corner of the rest house Min Min sees Pan Nyo, the daub of *thanaka* on her cheek visible by candlelight. Her long hair hangs loose over her shoulders. It makes her look younger and even cuter.

"Hey, we got a guest."

Pan Nyo sees Min Min. Her eyes go wide with surprise, then she breaks into a lovely approving smile. "I'm amazed you know this place."

"Sure, I know it."

"Of course he does. What's so difficult?" the chubby drummer girl butts in.

Beside them is an old woman, holding the last of a cigar. She looks at them with sleepy half-closed eyes and cups her hand to her ear.

"Grandma's hard of hearing. Her eyes aren't so good either. She's over eighty," volunteers Pan Nyo, savoring her dried fruit. Then leaning over to the old woman, she speaks up. "Grandma, this big brother gave us fried chicken and lots of money at a big house yesterday. Maung Lon brought him here tonight."

Just now, Pan Nyo said "big brother." An endearment that could mean many different things, though when she has to repeat it for her grandmother, she blushes. At her tender age, he can just imagine what's going through her mind.

"Pan Nyo, I wanted to treat you all to supper. Let's go to the food stalls, c'mon."

Pan Nyo's face brightens for one brief moment, then she shakes her head.

"We don't have any good clothes. You want to be seen with us?"

"Why not? What's the matter?" The girl tugs at Min Min's heartstrings. "Who sees clothes at night? The big singing star wants to dress up, does she?"

Pan Nyo smiles and looks down at her feet. Her young brother, Maung Lon, looks at Min Min and asks, "How 'bout me, can I come too?"

Min Min nods.

"Mi Pyon, you coming along?" Pan Nyo asks the drummer girl, then looks at her grandmother.

"Grandma, we're going to have supper at the food stalls. Supper. *Sup-per*." Mi Pyon sidles up close and still has to shout three or four times. Only then does the old woman nod and say, "Don't be late."

"C'mon, let's go."

Min Min and the boy start on ahead. Their poor neighbors are either already asleep or huddled over bowls of rice and curry.

"I don't want to go too far, okay?"

The slight worry in Pan Nyo's voice makes Min Min glance back. Look at her, she's using an old *longyi* to cover her head.

"What's this for? Let's lose it." Min Min pulls away the rag.

"No, I feel naked. I can't go out in public with my face uncovered."

Pan Nyo tries to grab the cloth from Min Min, but he just rolls it up and tosses it away in the dark. "There, all gone. Tomorrow Big Bro will get you a new one, okay?"

Her long mussed-up hair and shamed, simple face arouse Min Min. If the boy, Maung Lon, and drummer girl, Mi Pyon, weren't along it would be even better. Min Min grabs Pan Nyo by the hand and leads her into the festival market crowds. The trembling little fingers pretend to resist, but don't shake him off.

What would happen if Madame Hassle saw us now? It's too scary to think about. No, please, let's not think about Daisy. Let's just enjoy this pleasant moment.

"So, tell me what you want to eat. Milk tea and griddle cakes? Fried noodles?"

Min Min tries to convince the three of them to come sit down in a food stall, but they refuse. They just want to eat soup noodles from a hawker on the street. So while they slurp their noodles, Min Min trots off for a quick drink and a quid of betel.

"Hey, Min Min."

Min Min is thrown for a start. Oh, no, it's Ngwe Khin— Ngwe Khin! Good thing she didn't see me at the hawker's just now.

"So you got the old lady drunk, did you? Got a date? You can tell me."

"Please, don't go looking for trouble. I was feeling bored and I stepped out. Even at your age, you're always out on the prowl."

"Out and about, oh yes. Love never gets old, we *natkadaws* are always young for that. If I can't find a partner tonight, you'll do. Shall we?"

"Go away." Min Min pushes him off and runs. Can't stay around here, it's too dangerous. No escaping Madame Hassle's ilk.

"Let's go back. Grandma's expecting us," says Pan Nyo as soon as she sees Min Min. Now he's grateful to her. He knows they can't stay around here.

"Want anything else to eat? Did you have enough? Want any dried fruit?"

"No, thanks. We're okay, I had plenty."

On the way back, Min Min walks at a little distance from Pan Nyo and the others. He mustn't forget that among painted faces are many who know Daisy Bond.

"Big Bro, you spent a lot of money on us."

"Not so much."

*Now* the quiet girl wants to talk. Just when they have to get away quick.

"Tomorrow, I'll come sing at Big Bro's house, that song you requested."

"What song?"

" 'To Whom It May Concern,' remember?"

Such an innocent girl. Min Min had already forgotten, but she really means it.

"Pan Nyo, where did you learn so many songs? Who taught you?"

"Just my own interest. I used to sing along when they played music over the village loudspeakers."

A breeze bears the scent of flower offerings from the *nat* huts out to the open fields. The floral fragrances and distant *nat* music add a note of excitement. The scent of the girl, of a real woman, makes Min Min even more excited.

"How many brothers and sisters do you have, Pan Nyo?"

"Just us three."

"So you're the eldest?"

"Yes."

"And your father and mother?"

Pan Nyo goes quiet for a moment. "Papa and Mama broke up. Mama stayed with us for a while, then she left and never came back."

"So you don't sing out of choice."

"I don't know. I'm happy when I sing, but back home in our own village we wash clothes and do farm work. We only do songs at festivals. Grandma didn't used to let us work at all. She supported us by working as a maid in people's houses."

*A maid in people's houses.* The words sadden him. His own mother used to work for rich families to support Min Min and his brothers and sisters before she died.

"But you make enough money, right?"

"I guess. People give us what they feel like."

"Well, you do stir up feelings."

Min Min stops in the shadows before reaching the rest house. Maung Lon and Mi Pyon are already there.

"You're also very cute." Min Min pulls Pan Nyo to him. Drink makes him impulsive. Will she be his tonight? Min Min forces a kiss onto her virgin cheek.

"No, please don't. Not like this." Her voice is muffled, frightened, as if she's going to faint. Min Min repents and lets her go. Pan Nyo backs away, shaking all over.

Min Min quickly takes Pan Nyo by the hand. "I love you, Pan Nyo."

"You've been drinking." Pan Nyo's tearful voice trembles.

"Just a little. At the procession this evening, U Min Kyaw made me drink. Tell me, Pan Nyo, don't you like your big bro?"

The girl doesn't withdraw her hand. Min Min knows how to read girls and when to make moves. He pulls her toward him and kisses her on the cheek again.

"Are you and the old *natkadaw* related?" The girl's words explode in Min Min's ear. His hand drops away of itself. In the dark, Min Min sees her honest face waiting for his reply.

"U Ba Si's my brother. Not blood relations; we're like cousins twice removed."

"And what is it you do for him?"

The girl's question pierces his skin like a needle.

"I'm his . . . manager. I arrange his processions and stuff, whatever he needs."

"Oh, I see." She nods, accepting his explanation without question.

Min Min feels bad, but at least she's encouraging him. He

could brave anything with her by his side. He imagines them married for real and kisses her softly.

"I love you." This time, the words come from deep down inside. True words, not like all the *I love you*'s he's uttered to gays and girls alike. Please believe, this time it's different, Pan Nyo.

**6**

# HUNTING DAY

"LO, THE TWO LORD BROTHERS BY THEIR POWERS
created this oasis of freedom to give us total expiation and release these seven days. Though this life be burdened by financial straits and social commitments, though anger, ignorance,
and greed plague the mind, they give ease and repose. The
Lords grant us leave. Let all be happy, free in mind and body."

Fair, tall, and slender, tastefully made-up, rising star *natkadaw*
Thin Kyaing wears a plain, mauve silk, long-sleeved blouse
over a purple silk chambray *longyi*, and a lilac scarf tied smartly
at the neck. Daisy Bond gazes incredulously, listening to Thin
Kyaing's strange spiel.

What's he saying? The highfalutin words are in a new ora-
tory style the old Bond Girl can't follow. Okay, the fucker
knows fancy words because he's educated. Barely thirty, so-
called Princess Thin Kyaing just came on the scene this last

couple of years. A "Julia Roberts" in *natkadaw* circles, his *nat* hut is five or six rooms big, built on a huge lot. He has scores of devotees, some sleeping, some eating, some preparing offering trays or consulting the spirits with him. Too busy even for Daisy, he bows—*Wait a second, Mommy*—and goes on preaching while his loverboy serves tea-leaf salad and snacks.

The boy's not bad either. Handsome face, wispy mustache like a Bollywood movie star. Thin Kyaing's probably tutored him special: He doesn't come close or even talk to Daisy, but just busies himself with other things. Others' boys are so accomplished. See how well-behaved he is compared to hers? That little fucker Min came back at three in the morning, then went out again right after breakfast. He's got paying guests. Who has time to be traipsing through the woods asking after him? Wherever he's gone, it can only lead to trouble. Man troubles up to here.

Daisy's had to stop him before, had to spy on him so many times. Can't live without him, so now he's chasing all over the jungle after the bastard, checking his haunts. He's checked Hla Thuza Mae's whore hut, been to see that woman Ma Khin Htay who always wears low-cut blouses and bends over when she throws dice. They didn't dare stop him. He shouted them down, looked behind their curtains, threatened them with mortal peril and *nat* curses. He even went looking for that damn Moneypenny Ngwe Khin. Who knows where the loose leaf is blowing about at this early hour? In one hut and out the next, talk about tiring. By the time he got to Thin Kyaing's hut, he had to ask for a bottle of soda water. It's his karma to bear. What's a *meinmasha* to do?

"Untrustworthy friends and scoundrels cheat you? Never fear. You'll get back your smile, your Lord will help you recover your losses, okay? Here, keep this scarf with you always to triumph over whomever wrongs you."

Nice delivery. Must be why he's so popular. Daisy looks on skeptically as a woman humbly accepts an orange scarf from Thin Kyaing, a cigarette poised just so on his pale pink lips. Thin Kyaing eyes Daisy knowingly through the smoke.

"And what day is it today?"

"It's Hunting Day, my Lord."

"Right, today is the day to hunt hares for Kodawgyi and Kodawlei. The day to catch rabbits and hares. We two Brothers always manifest in human form to drink palm wine in Taungbyon. One day, the palm orchard patron offered us grilled hare to go with our palm wine. It was so tasty, we called him over and asked, *What's this meat, old man?* When we learned what it was, we transformed back into *nats* and commanded that people offer us grilled hare whenever we appear in Taungbyon. One time, however, a woman let loose all the hares that were to be served us. When the time came for us to appear and there was no hare meat, we flew into a rage and commenced to swear up and down. Young and hot-blooded, weren't we?

"Now, two days before every Taungbyon Festival full moon is Hunting Day. One village has to catch hares and grill the meat on spits, and on the way to the Palace to offer these skewers, they can swear at anybody however much they like. They *must* swear. Moreover, those cursed at should not get mad, because the more one profanes or is profaned on this day, the more one's fortunes will increase the whole year. The grilled hare offerings should be arriving at the Palace any minute now, so go and get yourselves cursed! You over there, Lady-in-waiting Daisy, aren't you going to get cursed?"

Ha! Thin Kyaing, you think you're so clever! The name is Bond, Daisy Bond. You know me better than that. Every *natkadaw* alive has heard of my Hunting Day exploits. When this Bond Girl was young and rambunctious, I'd go to the Palace and wait for the villagers to come offer their hare meat. I stood in everyone's way—man, woman, and child. It was so much fun, especially with the pious elders. They were so timid, so scared to swear out loud, they hardly moved their mouths. I made such a scene, tickling and teasing. Shocked them into swearing for real.

"Nay, my Lord, I'm not much for hot air. I do things direct." Let's just see how your eyes bulge now, Jumped-up Julia!

Actually, as a Minister, I'm supposed to be at the Grand Palace right now with all the turban-wearing big shots to receive the hare meat, but dear Daisy's so caught up in her boy chase, how can I go?

Thin Kyaing ignores Daisy's remark. "Come up front and bow. You want to put out a stereo recording, right?"

A young girl comes forward and hands Thin Kyaing five two-hundred-kyat bills. Thin Kyaing puts the money to his forehead and bows.

"Here we have an artiste. Dedicate yourself, voice and body, that all who see your face and hear your voice be enamored. That you might triumph over your competition."

Well, well, so the brat knows how to pray. Maybe I should steal his style. Such a big fucking hero just because he's been making offerings to the *nats* since he was still in shorts. It's almost unfair; he has the advantage of coming from a *natkadaw* family. The brat's uncle is a *natkadaw* and gay, too. Guess *meinmashas* run in the family. He's been running off to dance at his uncle's *nat* ceremonies since he started school. Even when his family found out, they couldn't stop him. No one who enters this path ever turns back.

Okay, the brat has things going for him. At one *nat* ceremony when his uncle was dancing U Min Kyaw's spirit, he just went up and danced. He was just a child and still didn't know the rules—U Min Kyaw doesn't share the stage with anyone. Such daring, the audience was in awe. Since then, audiences have eaten him up. He was in eighth grade at the time and still wearing green school shorts.

Tells a good story, too. Like about when he held his own first *nat* ceremony. What a laugh! One day he went to a friend's beauty parlor at Bogyok Aung San Market in Yangon to cruise for boys. And who does he meet but gemstone-trader ladies from Mogok. And they have a very precious stone they can't move. Finally they decide to consult the *nats*, but gay friends at the beauty parlor advise them, *Don't go to big-name* natkadaws, *they're going to cost you. Better you should ask this girl,* they say, *she's like this with the* nats. *Just ask, don't pay a thing till you get results.* So Thin Kyaing says they'll never sell it in Yangon, they have to sell the stone back where they got it. After that, if they succeed, they should hold a three-day *nat* ceremony.

Okay, they say. They go back up to Mandalay and the stone sells just like that. So to keep their promise, they come back to Yangon and lay out twenty thousand kyats for a ceremony. This was back when a three-day do only cost eight thousand kyats, so twenty thousand kyats was no small sum. Thin Kyaing was so happy, he gives ten thousand to his uncle to arrange everything for a three days and spends the entire remaining ten thousand shopping for clothes. Come the day, her damn uncle gets the date wrong. No dance stage, no uncle. There he was, crying at his first ceremony. But the gem-trader ladies say, okay, let the child use the money, they're satisfied. The following morning, her uncle arrives with a big truckload of supplies to set the stage and prepare for the ceremony. But he forgets the food and drink to offer to the *nats,* so he has to go and pawn his rings to get five hundred kyats for offerings. Compared to all that, *nat* possession was a breeze.

Still, the brat doesn't have any followers or experience. The gem traders' companions, rich wives from Mandalay, they think the ceremony is off and had already booked berths on the train for that day. They're just getting ready to leave when he gets up to dance. All at once he's talking in tongues, *You there, I won't let you go! Just try to leave, you'll be back. Nobody's going to Mandalay today.* They leave anyway, but before long their cab drives up again. Thin Kyaing himself is startled. As it turns out, they'd forgotten a key, left it with one of the gem traders still at the ceremony. That's why they came back. But the thing is, his prophecy really came true. Since then, those rich folk have flocked to him.

After that, the brat turned pro. He talks modern and explains things more convincingly than other *natkadaws*. He persuades educated people, his devotees are a cut above the rest.

"A *nat* permeates like mist, adheres to the body and shakes it, yet the mind never strays or passes out. If a *natkadaw* were unaware or didn't know what was going on, that would be deceit. How could a spirit not know when it's in someone?"

There, that kind of smarts, talking clever circles. Look, he's even got that *nat* maven in the audience nodding.

"During the reign of King Mindon, the Court banned the Taungbyon Festival. They said that *natkadaws* were fakirs, that *nat* possession was a sham. Even under King Thibaw, the Festival remained banned. When did it start up again? During British colonial times. Since then, the festival has grown year by year. Bigger and bigger crowds come to worship the *nats*. Why? Because human life is fraught with problems, social duties, and financial straits. People need something to believe in, to depend on, right? But when the British reinstated Taungbyon, they had an agenda. They weren't thinking about the happiness of the people or the country at all. No such good intentions. We Burmese were downtrodden and disgraced, enslaved by the British. We all hated the Brits, so the Crown sought to create a diversion. They saw how we love festivities and entertainment, how easily we're distracted. The timing was perfect. We missed our deposed king, we longed to beseech royalty, and the only Lords around were at Taungbyon. People missed the Palace and the Court, the Queen Mothers, Ministers, and Royal Guards—titles now used only at Taungbyon. The British sought to placate us by using our *natkadaws* as stooges. They didn't reinstate Taungbyon for *natkadaws* to cheat people, they reinstated Taungbyon to cheat the country. *Nats* are real, but what about *natkadaws*? Our Mommy Daisy here always says a *natkadaw* gets run around the pot of hell, isn't that right?"

Daisy mouths a silent *Fuck you, Thin Kyaing.* Clever is clever, but he sure as hell is long-winded. I just came for a clue about that fucker Min's whereabouts, and this brilliant fucker keeps me waiting forever.

One follower speaks up. "Thin Kyaing, about your spell just now to avert misfortune, where should I go to perform my vows?"

"Any Wish-Fulfilling Pagoda. The proper offering consists of bananas, a coconut, and a bunch of red roses. If there's no Wish-Fulfilling Pagoda near your house, you can do it here at the one in Taungbyon. Even better, if you want to leave me your five-hundred-fifty-kyat offering, I'll go there first thing in the morning. What'll it be?"

The woman fishes a few bills from a large sack of money to give to Thin Kyaing, who wedges them into the bananas on the altar with feigned disinterest.

"Thank you, Thin Kyaing. I'll be leaving."

"Everything's going to be fine. Don't worry about a thing," says Julia Roberts with a nasal lilt, then stands up and walks over to Daisy.

"So you're going to get up at the crack of dawn and go to the Pagoda, are you?" Thin Kyaing shoots him a nasty *mein-masha* glare. "You've got so much time, Mommy, you go. You know I never get up early."

The two of them slap hands and laugh.

"So tell me, what can I do for you? Want something to eat, Mommy? Hey, Hpo Chit, bring me a Pepsi."

"There you go with Hpo Chit again. Be happy while you can. Look, I don't want anything to eat or drink, Thin Kyaing. Just answer me a question or two."

"It's about your boy-o, isn't it?"

"Right. This morning, did you see him around? Or even yesterday? What do you hear? Tell me anything you know."

Thin Kyaing lights a cigarette and fans Daisy's heart with his hand. "You're burning up, Mommy. Wherever he went, whatever he's done, he'll be back. You've got your livelihood to think of; why drop everything and go chasing after him?"

"No, I've got to look for him. This burns like nothing else. You're so cool, how can I expect you to sympathize?"

"Really. You think I've never been on fire? All us gays have our time in heat."

"Well, if you know what it's like, stop making fun of me. You obviously don't know anything, so I'm gone. I've got to find Ngwe Khin."

"Hold on, Mommy. I'll have Hpo Chit go look. No need to chase Ngwe Khin down yourself."

"No, that'll take time. Better go myself."

Daisy Bond stands up and storms off. Where can that loose-leaf Moneypenny be? Every lane and alleyway is teeming with people, it's enough to infuriate anyone. Damn you, Min, when I catch you, first thing I'm going to do is slap you on the cheek. Then I'll rub your nose in the dirt and take back all my jewelry. You give me such trouble, you're trying to kill me.

"Yoo-hoo, Daisy, lose your boy again?" That snide voice can only be Ngwe Khin. There's the troublemaker, with his batik shirt and cigarette, in someone else's hut.

"Come here. I've been looking all over for you. I got stuff to ask you, fatherfucker."

Ngwe Khin stands up calmly and doesn't even bother to curse back. "Don't ask me about your little prick. Just a waste of breath. Let me buy you another one. I know of one little boy, not too pricey. Leave me some money and I'll buy him for you."

"Yeah right, Mother dearest. Like I don't know you'd mother the boy yourself. Just tell me what you hear about Min Min. You see him anywhere last night?"

Ngwe Khin lets on nothing but his own brand of emotionless ennui.

"Oh, not that again. Out with it, Your Ladyship, any juicy little drippings."

"What difference would it make if I told you? It's been ages since you could control the kid anyway. He'll be back to the hitching post when the time comes."

"You know me too well, Ngwe Khin. Just tell me where the fucker is. You know every whore hut there is."

"He's not anyplace I know of. Your number's doing things on the sly. With a good girl, not some sleaze. Don't ask me who. Last night I only saw them from far off," Ngwe Khin reports objectively. "That's all I know, okay?"

Daisy droops. Right there in the festival lane, the famous *natkadaw* starts to tremble and shake uncontrollably as if really possessed. "And you don't have a clue? With all the people you know?"

"What a pain. I *told* you I don't know."

"May the *nats* strike you, kill you cold?"

"Cold as told."

"How old was she?"

"No more than seventeen or eighteen. You need to ask? A kid who lives with an old lady pushing sixty's bound to run off with someone his own age."

Daisy focuses all his frustration on Ngwe Khin in a stream of invective. Unperturbed, Moneypenny merely hears him out while selectively fine-tuning the most debilitating words to toss back.

"Don't swear at me. You'll just rouse your musty old sandalwood smell."

Daisy fumes, then turns to leave.

"Hold it right there. Pay me for my report."

"Yeah right, a coin in your mouth for your passage to the next world."

Daisy leaves Ngwe Khin laughing and storms off all hot and bothered, not even looking back when anyone says hello. Damn you, Min, how many times have you hurt me? I've told you nicely, sworn up and down, warned you every which way. I thought you might feel a little affection for me, but now you kick me in the chest.

"Daisy."

Somebody grabs him by the hand. Now who? Daisy is almost in tears, but his nose detects a strong alcohol smell. It's that boozer Master Nat Maung, wearing a faded shirt and *longyi*, bloodshot eyes and puffy face, his unoiled red hair in a mess. In his day, the Master was a smooth-talking superstar the women all adored.

Holding tight with one hand, he rubs the rings on Daisy's makeup-coated fingers with the other. "Pocketbook Daisy, you look so beautiful. Give ol' Nat Maung some money, love, he hasn't had a bite to eat."

Oh *dokka!* Just when I've got things to do, the old boy burbles, a mere caricature of the heartthrob he used to be. How officials' wives and rich ladies fell for him—me too, to tell the truth. He still wasn't gay when he first came on the scene. Tall and fair and handsome in trousers. Either white slacks with a white shirt or white slacks with a brown shirt, he looked sharp. The women were crazy about Nat Maung, his *nat* hut was always full. But between women, cards, drink, and drugs, he really screwed himself. Unfaithful and undisciplined, he ended in the gutter and lost his name. He whored himself and became a total alcoholic. He's in a bad way now, begging from one hut to another, drinking up whatever he gets, sleeping wherever. Daisy feels sorry for him; the poor fuck's going to meet his death like this.

"Here's some money. Isn't much, but I'm in a hurry. I got lots to do at home."

Nat Maung stuffs the fifteen-kyat bill into his ragged pocket, but doesn't let go of Daisy's hand. "Wait. Let ol' Nat Maung give you a kiss."

"No, no—no kisses. Take your hands off me. Beat it. Scram."

Daisy struggles free and runs, scared to wind up like Nat

Maung. Well, that's karma. The gay life carries such heavy karma. Min, honey, I'm going to pay off all my debts to you in this life. Oh, to clear up all my karma this time around!

As soon as Daisy steps inside his gate, he hears shouting. "Here she is, here's Daisy!" It's a whole slew of his *nat* followers.

"When did you all arrive? Come tell me." He wants to cry, but pretends to smile, wiping all traces of grief from his professional face. All in a day's work. "You there, rich lady, don't be pouting. Did you bring *longyis* for the Lords? I'm sure I told you last year, didn't I?" Daisy churns out pandering words as he walks, when just then Ahpongyi appears at the kitchen door and points upstairs with a spoon. Daisy's heart leaps in his chest. The fucker's upstairs. So he came back, did he?

There's that sweet voice that can shake a Bond Girl's heart, a voice so skilled at keeping the customers happy. "Yes, yes, very good. Please be sure to tell her and she'll do it. Ah, here she comes now." Then as soon as Daisy enters, Min Min adds, "They've been waiting for ages."

Acting like nothing's happened, so sweet and innocent, the young fucker.

"So tell me what's on your mind. Quick now. I stepped out with my own husband troubles and now I'm exhausted."

The women roar with laughter. They know Daisy Bond very well. Min Min just smiles and plays dumb. He goes to get Daisy a soft drink and a straw.

"It's so hard to find a good squeeze these days."

Daisy's followers laugh again, but Min Min fires him a warning glance. *Cut the crap and get on with business.*

Okay, okay. I'll do my bit and run around the pot of hell to keep you in fancy clothes, food, and women. "Tell me, what days of the week were you both born?"

"He's Tuesday-born and I'm Thursday-born."

"Well, Tuesday and Thursday go together in business; your fortunes and holdings will rise like the tide. Yes, Lords Bobogyi and Bobolei, on behalf of this Tuesday-born son and Thursday-born daughter, your servant regularly offers money for flowers, mirrors, perfume, and robes. Let their hair be a carpet beneath your feet, my Lords. Feed them, make them rich and beautiful. Starting here and now, give their whole family—one and all—health, wealth, and ease in personal relations."

"Please, I've got a business deal coming up within a week."

"Keep this flametree twig and sprig of eugenia for when you talk business, and they'll make you triumph. When it comes through, you'll have to offer a procession next year, you hear?"

"I will, I promise."

"The king keeps his royal precepts and the people keep their word, isn't that right? You, the lady over there, what day were you and your husband born?"

"We're both Sunday-born, and our sons are Saturday, Friday, and Monday. Please pray for us to do well financially, for me to get a promotion, for all my sons to pass their exams, and help us buy a car."

"Fine. You want a lot, but you're offering the *nats* forty-five kyats?"

"Just for the lucky number nine, Daisy, that's all."

"Well, if you really want a lucky multiple of nine, just offer nine ninety-kyat bills. Here's your forty-five kyats back, so now give me five ninety-kyats."

"Sure, no problem."

Daisy is starting to sweat from all this showmanship, but someone is fanning him. Well, the boy is good at pampering when he feels like it. Daisy would work for him tirelessly if he'd just stay like this and never leave.

"Don't forget next year after you succeed, okay? The king keeps his royal precepts, the people keep their word. May you come and go in peace, safe and free from harm."

The group clears out. Daisy lies down on his rattan pillow, exhausted in mind and body, while Min Min counts the offering money. "Where were you?" he asks. "Everyone was waiting for you."

Ha, listen to the sneak! In front of others he acts so sweet, but turn their backs and he changes face. Daisy sits up angrily. Shouldn't pick fights on Hunting Day, but swearing is perfectly in order. "I went out looking for *you*, fucker. I don't go chasing about for fun. You're the one who nipped out last night to go sleep with some girl."

"Stop talking nonsense. I had things to do. Who tells you these things?"

"People see what they see. I got it firsthand, Ngwe Khin saw you very clearly."

"Ha, there you go. You believe Ngwe Khin? That's a laugh. You always say never believe a third of what Ngwe Khin says."

That shuts Daisy up. It's true. Ngwe Khin can't be a third trusted. That cunt should make him feel so unhappy! Gets him so wound up, he can't tell what's what. Same difference, really. Min lies just as much as Ngwe Khin. Still, Daisy has to smile as he watches Min Min methodically readying the offerings for this evening.

Another group files upstairs, joking about all the Hunting Day profanities.

"Get yourself cursed? Got it nice and dirty, did you?"

The unmarried girls in the group squeal in protest.

"Hey, don't be shy. Today the two Lords forgive us whatever we say, however rude we act. The cruder the better, the more lucky money'll come your way."

A fat woman with shiny glasses and diamond earrings leads the group in, and everyone bows respectfully to Daisy Bond's antique *nat* turban on the altar.

"Daisy Bond, please summon the two Lords, Shwepyingyi and Shwepyinlei."

She offers five ninety-kyat bills. Daisy raises the money to his forehead, mumbles a recitation, then stuffs it between the bananas in the offering bowl. Then he bows and invokes the spirits until his praying hands start to shake and hit himself on the forehead.

"Yo, approach your Lord. Saturday-born heiress, you remain true to your Lord?"

"Yes, my Lord, we're here."

Daisy wobbles in place, his eyes glaze over.

"Hey, little brother, gimme a smoke."

Min Min offers him two cigarettes and a soft drink.

"This is the butterfly master's beloved little brother."

Daisy does it again, embarrassing Min Min in front of his laughing lady followers. No way to fade back gracefully, he'd just call him up nearby. One good thing, though, this *nat* only drinks juice. With an alcoholic spirit, he'd really be in for it.

"Hey, little brother. What's this cigarette?"

"It's a Duya, m'Lord. Export quality Duya."

"Here, Duchess. If you want things to go special, smoke this Duya from my lips. Give me the other one, little brother."

"Here's a Kabaung cigarette, m'Lord."

"That's the ticket. Listen, Duchess, if you want people to act respectful, you have to smoke my Kabaung. I'm the one lifting you, see?"

"Yes, my Lord, and please lift me higher. I want to come to you in a brand-new car, but business was so slow this past year, I couldn't even trade in my old car."

"Go home now and that new car is yours. Satisfied?"

"Yes, my Lord."

"And when you get your new car, don't forget your Lord. You're to offer two long rolls of *longyi* material and six scarves, you hear?"

"Yes, my Lord."

"Hey, little brother, fan your Lord."

"This little sister also wants to fan her Lord," jokes one woman. She almost steals the fan away from Min Min, when Shwepyingyi's spirit slams Daisy's hand flat on the floor.

"I don't want anybody else, just him!"

The entire audience bursts out laughing. Min Min accommodates with a smile and resigns himself to fanning duty.

Infused with Shwepyingyi's aura, Daisy casts him a loving look and raises the soft drink to his lips, when just then—

> *To whom it may concern*
> *I send my love and yearn*
> *For your swift and safe return*
> *To whom I now address*
> *May this bring you happiness*
> *Silver smiles and gold success . . .*

A sweet, plaintive voice floats over the fence. Min Min's fanning hand wavers, but Shwepyingyi holds the drink aloft and continues preaching, oblivious to the song.

> *. . . I parcel out my heart and care*
> *It may take months, it may take years*
> *Let love breeze from here to there*
> *To whom it may concern, my dear . . .*

Min Min drops the fan. If only Daisy would close his eyes and keep trance-talking.

> *. . . Always hoping*
> *Always wishing*
> *Always waiting . . .*

Shwepyingyi opens Daisy's eyes to find the spirit's little brother nowhere near. Where did he go? Did an important guest show up?

"My Lord, this Tuesday-born daughter is supposed to go work abroad in the next few months. Is it sure? Does foreign travel figure in my future?"

"Tuesday-born, did you say?" Shwepyingyi stands up abruptly.

> . . . *After all*
> *So far, so long*
> *Will you recall*
> *My voice, my song?* . . .

Only now does the singing and hand-clapping reach Daisy's ears. "Which day was that? Oh, right, a Tuesday-born daughter who wants to go abroad."

Puffing pretentiously on Shwepyingyi's cigarette, Daisy glances out over the fence to see a bright red scarf on the singing girl's head. And smiling beside her, Shwepyingyi's little brother, Daisy's own darling Min! Shwepyingyi shakes Daisy violently. I know what you're up to, Min, I know every last smutty detail. Ngwe Khin's an old friend, she takes my side, she doesn't lie to me. You're the liar, you're the cheat. Any real female who comes along, rich or poor, you just can't keep away. How dare you—Daisy Bond's boy with a beggar girl! Stealing my favorite scarf to give to the likes of her! Disgraceful, my scarf is tainted. Shwepyingyi barely contains his rage as Daisy's mind leaps up, rips the scarf off the girl's head, and tears it to pieces.

"My Lord, so will this Tuesday-born daughter go abroad?"

Shwepyingyi turns away from the window, reeling and swaying.

> . . . *Two together hand in hand*
> *Living together heart to heart* . . .

Shwepyingyi throws the soft drink against the wall. Daisy falls to the floor rolling and screaming, "No! I'm not hearing this! Get that beggar away from my gate now!"

# 7

# TREE-
# CHOPPING
# CEREMONY

THE AUGUST MOON SPREADS ITS LIGHT IN ALL DIREC-
tions around the rest house but scarcely penetrates the trees
shading the two trysting lovers. Min Min holds Pan Nyo's
hand, silk scarf sparkling around her neck in the dappled
moonlight. She really likes the scarf, he thinks. No one's ever
given her anything like this before.

"This *tein* wood will bring us lots of money, right?"

"You bet. It's good for business, brings in customers."

"But my family and me, we don't have a business."

Min Min laughs. "Your little singing group *is* a business,
silly."

Pan Nyo holds up the tiny piece of *tein* wood to the moon
and examines it.

"We watched them chopping the *tein* trees last year, but
from far away. There were so many people fighting for pieces.

We could see the sharp knives, but they all rushed in anyway. This wood, did you have to fight people to get it?"

"Not us, the chief celebrant who chops the branches brought it to us after offering it to the two Lords. People especially want this blessed wood for business."

"But why cut *tein* trees?"

"Well, the story goes that the Brothers' godfather, King Anawrahta, cut down a *tein* tree where a spirit was living, so the angry *tein* tree spirit took the form of a buffalo and gored the king to death. That's why the Brothers hate *tein* trees, and why one festival day's set aside to chop down *tein* trees. On that day, they plant *tein* branches around the Palace for the Chief Celebrant to go into a trance and whack them all to pieces for offerings. If people get hurt when the Chief Celebrant swings his knives, it's not his fault. They don't care. They just hear it's lucky and rush right in."

"That's horrible."

Pan Nyo undoes the scarf from her neck and carefully knots one corner, then ties it neatly around her neck again. She's so pleased with her new plaything. How happy would she be if she heard Madame Hassle squawk? Screaming that Pan Nyo doesn't deserve this long-outmoded scrap of a scarf now tainted by Pan Nyo's skin? U Ba Si swore his Hunting Day head off. Min Min had to argue and coax and shout, use every persuasion in the book to get him to calm down. The poor girl sang well, so he gave her some money and food, so what? What's an old rag from the bottom of a trunk? It wasn't to win the girl's affections. If he doesn't want to believe him, fine.

Of course Min Min knew Daisy wouldn't buy it, but he stayed put all night and the whole day today just to keep him happy. Not that Daisy lets down his guard even when he's in a good mood. Come evening, while Daisy was busy with customers after a Lesser Shrine procession, somehow Min Min made his way here. Well, at least U Min Kyaw had him drink himself drowsy. Just hope he stays asleep.

"This afternoon, people at another *nat* hut kept requesting songs. They gave us lots of money, and rice and curry, too."

"So you didn't come visit us because you got lots of money?"

"No, don't you remember what you said? You told me not to come around because your brother *natkadaw* doesn't like to hear singing when he's in a trance."

"Ah yes, that's right."

The poor girl is so innocent. So simply she entangles him.

"Bro, *natkadaws* have it good, don't they?"

"How's that?"

"I mean, *natkadaw* work sounds wonderful. I'd like to be a *natkadaw*."

What is she saying?

"Well, a *natkadaw* just dresses up and puts on makeup. Comfortable life, nothing very tiring. I guess the *nats* aren't with me, though, maybe because we don't have money."

"It's not like that."

"No, it must be. This one rice-porridge vendor here in Taungbyon, she wanted to stop selling porridge and become a *natkadaw*, but the *nats* didn't want her. The *nats* only lift people from far away."

"What's this all about?"

Pan Nyo laughs softly and leans on Min Min's shoulder.

"Just one more festival day left tomorrow."

"Yeah."

"Bro, where will you go? Next year will you—?"

"Not even next year. I'll see you in between."

"You'll what?" Pan Nyo pulls back suddenly and looks at Min Min in disbelief. "You mean you want to come with me?"

Poor girl. Min Min squeezes Pan Nyo's hand compassionately.

"You want to stay together with me?"

"Of course I do. Big Bro'll stay together with you, Pan Nyo."

Why is he saying this? He never intended to say anything of the kind.

"I love you, Bro."

Pan Nyo, your innocent voice puts me to shame. Forgive me, my life isn't so pure and innocent. Min Min kisses Pan Nyo's hand softly, when just then—

*Hey, Min!*

A voice that shakes the moon and trees. Min Min drops Pan Nyo's hand.

"Min, where are you? Come out right now."

He's here. He's followed him to finish off the last of Min Min's life.

"Min, dear. I'm calling you, can't you hear?"

I eat what he feeds me, I accept what he gives me, I do

whatever he wants me to. His obedient five-hundred-kyat slave. Should I listen?

"Hey, I'm shouting, aren't you fucking ashamed? You shameless prick, come out. Where are you sleeping with that husband-thieving beggar?"

Min Min stands up brusquely. Pan Nyo shakes all over, holding on to Min Min's hand even as he pushes her away.

"You . . . you're the *natkadaw*'s—?" Her quavering voice sends terror through him.

"Hey, Min dear!"

"Go, Pan Nyo, just go."

Min Min emerges from the shadows. The rest-house poor folk peer out at them.

"Listen, everyone, here's a man who has to put on makeup and paint his lips to make a living. I work my ass off just to feed this shameless prick and he steals from my offering bowl to go chasing after women, think about it!" The moon spotlights Daisy Bond's furious face smudged with makeup. His unruly hair stripped of a hairpiece, a long pearl necklace swinging over a silver flare-waisted dancer's jacket, the shame artist's white-hot eyes bulge between fake lashes. "I said come out! Go and beg with that beggar for all I care. Just give me my things!"

Daisy's myopic eyes are too blurred with emotion to see him approach. Out of nowhere, Min Min grabs him by the arm. "Shut your trap, or I'll hit you."

"Hit me, will you? I'll shut up when I want. Now I'm shouting, okay? Hey, everyone!" Min Min covers Daisy's mouth with his hand and drags him away panting hard. Min Min doesn't hear; he's listening for crying from the rest house. Angry and embarrassed and hurt, Min Min pulls the weak old *meinmasha* all the way home and lets him drop.

Daisy's ladylike wrist is red and sore, the silver jacket is torn at the shoulder. His scalp is sore. Oh Lord Buddha, did he drag him by the hair? He can't even remember getting here. He's so tired he can't breathe.

"My heart, my heart. Water. Please, some water."

Faithful Ahpongyi rushes out with a tin cup. He doesn't look once at Min Min. Heading back to the kitchen, he grits his teeth and pounds a clenched fist in his other hand.

"I'm so tired. I'm dying. He tried to kill me."

"What?" Min Min turns and glares. "You shame me and ruin my life, and now you accuse me? Typical *meinmasha* lies. Either you keep me under the covers or you keep me under lock and key like a common criminal. Like I'm stealing from you."

"Oh, you know all about us *meinmashas,* do you?" The feisty old Bond Girl sits up. "If we're as bad as all that, why stay with me? Nobody forced you."

"Back then I didn't know a thing. And once I did, I didn't want to stay."

"So you don't want to stay anymore? Now that you've eaten your fill of fatty flesh. You kick an old lady in the chest and you're off with some tender teen?"

"Yes, I've found myself a wife. I'm going to get married."

Min Min has never been so blunt. Daisy just stares at him, tears streaming down his cheeks. "No, you can't get married.

You must love me," sobs Daisy, hugging Min Min from behind. "Don't you love me anymore? I can't live without you. I'll die if you leave me. You'll just have to kill me."

"Oh, stop it." Min Min turns and stares at Daisy's crazed face running with red and blue and black makeup. "You say you love me. Did you ever think about things from my side? Do you realize how people see you *meinmashas*? They fear you, they loathe you. You disgust them. They avoid you when they see a *meinmasha* coming. Nobody wants you, not even your relations. Do you ever think how hard it is for me to go around with someone of the same sex? Do you realize how much courage it takes for me to stay with a *meinmasha?* You treat me like I'm living under your skirt. Well, maybe I am, but I don't drink all the time or demand fancy things. I work hard for my meals and my clothes. I help out a lot, I even take care of your skirts. Is that man's work? I can say this because I feel a kinship to you—not love or affection or desire. Maybe I felt those things when I was young and innocent, but now I know different. You're more like a brother or uncle. Now I want to get married, so please, let me go."

Daisy is afraid to look at Min Min. He's always done as he was told and never complained. "What have I done wrong? What have I ever done to you?"

"What have you *done*? What *haven't* you done? You know you're always saying, *Never hurt anyone. Anger goes away, but hurt never heals.* U Ba Si, you've hurt me so many times I can't even begin to count. You shame me in front of people. You swear at me in the middle of the fairway for any little thing that displeases you. You slap me on the cheek. Without any grounds, you accuse me of sleeping with whores, pull me out of other *nat* huts and parade my guilt around the whole festival. You shout me down, *Thief, thief!* Or have you forgotten? I was going to catch a bus to see my mother. This ring, this gold ring, remember? You told me not to wear it when I went to visit her because you were worried my poor mother might steal it. No, I begged you, I just wanted to look respectable. I promised nothing would happen to it. But you chased after me, shouting, *Anyone who takes my things without permission is a thief! A gold ring thief!* I remember it all. I remember everything you did to hurt me."

"I did it because I love you. I shamed you so you'd never do it again. Forget it already. What have I done to you lately? I gave you everything I have, right?"

"Your trusted slave. You had me scrimp and save every little scrap of food and clothing, that was your rule. And then I had to show you a list of everything I used."

"You were a simple country boy. You didn't even know how to fudge a list, you showed me an accurate inventory."

"I learned to lie because of you. You screwed me up."

"Okay, you win. Have your victory. I'm the villain."

"You're not losing much. You only paid five hundred kyats."

"Five hundred kyats was only the beginning. I paid with my heart. This heart of mine, that's my base cost. If I forfeit that, what's my life worth? I'm as good as dead." Daisy wheezes in anguish. "The way you talk, I'd have to ask your forgiveness for loving you. You who once hit me in the face because of a woman. My eyesight hasn't been the same since."

Min Min says nothing. Madame Bond rubs away the tears with spiteful effort.

"So now you're going to get married? All our *meinmasha* lives, we watch and wait and worry about this very thing. That one day you kick me in the chest and knock my eyes back in my head. Now I smell old to you, the love is gone. Like they say, *Fallen leaves are never rejoined, nor sweet dreams ever regained.* I know it's time to make a break. Fire melts steel, but it takes diamond to cut a diamond, iron to cut iron, so must a heart cut the heart. Very well, I'll break my heart to pieces."

More tears stream down Daisy's cheeks. "Last night I couldn't sleep. I just knew you and that girl were cheating on me. To think how in the past we ate together and drank together, had fun together, made donations together—the scenes rolled by like a movie. How you took care of me when I was sick, how you looked after me on trips. The tears kept me awake the whole night, so before dawn I got up and drank myself to sleep."

"Stop it. I told you, what's past is past. What lies ahead is what matters."

"You just don't want to think back. You don't want to remember because you're heartless. You hate me."

"I already told you, I feel close to you."

Daisy eyes him hopefully. "If you feel so close, why leave? Why can't you stay with me?"

"Look," Min Min cuts him short, "you're not a woman. You're a man with a woman's mind. How can I stay my whole life with you? You just don't understand."

"Maybe I don't, but the one thing I do understand is I'm a

woman. I speak, laugh, cry as a woman. I feel everything as a woman. That makes me a woman. I'm a woman inside."

"Say it till the day you die, you'll never be a woman. You're a fake and you know it."

Daisy plants his arms at his waist in a surge of James Bond pride. "Forget I said anything. You'd jilt me, more woman than most, for some simple country girl?"

"Hey, don't be rude. Have some manners."

"Oh yes, Mr. Manners, will you please answer the question? Who's the blushing bride-to-be, Your Highness?"

"Not that it's any of your business, I'm marrying Pan Nyo."

"Hold on. You'd marry a beggar and do what for her? Eat from her begging bowl?"

"I have arms and legs. I can work as a coolie. I can pedal a trishaw."

"Even if you had the strength to climb Mount Meru, you? Pedal a trishaw? Don't make me laugh. Look at me, Min." Madame Bond smirks. "You have it so soft because I work hard for you. A cush like you doing coolie labor? Think about it."

"You wait and see. I'm out of here. Here's your things back."

Daisy bends over in disbelief as Min Min drops all his jewelry on the carpet.

"Anyone who leaves gold chains and watches and bracelets and rings to go sweat his coolie ass off must be crazy."

"I'm not crazy. *You're* the crazy one."

"That's right, I'm a woman insane."

Min Min makes for the door. "I'm wearing the clothes you bought me, that's all."

Daisy tugs at Min Min's hand. "Min, darling."

"I'm going my own way. Step aside."

"No, I refuse."

"Out of my way!"

Min Min knocks him down and runs. Daisy just lies there dazed in the dark.

I'm coming, Pan Nyo. Big Bro Min Min is coming to stay with you forever.

# 8

## GILDING
## THE
## IMAGES

ON THE LAST DAY OF THE TAUNGBYON FESTIVAL, THE Queen Mothers, Chief Ministers, Ministers, and all the shrine staff are very busy at the Grand Palace. They gild the two Brothers' statues, then immediately dress them in new robes and scarves.

All the *natkadaws* are also busily preparing to leave for the Yatanagu Festival south of Mandalay where the two Brothers will escort their mother, Lady Popa, two weeks hence. *Natkadaws* who made money at Taungbyon can rest easy for a week, but it's time for loss leaders like Ngwe Khin to get cracking. There are deals to be made: Some will pawn their bowls to cover expenses, others their *nat* images and knives, their *longyis* and clothes. Maybe they lost at cards or drank up all their earnings or simply didn't make anything. Some were too far off the beaten track or just too unlucky to attract customers. Little-known *natkadaws* are sure to go broke.

They can buy back their things at the Yatanagu Festival. Either way, Moneypenny Ngwe Khin is running around from one *nat* hut to another. *Natkadaws* not only pawn their belongings, they also trade and sell husbands. This *natkadaw* wants to buy that young lad, that *natkadaw* needs to sell off this young guy, all deals to broker.

Some luckless *natkadaws* make a show of eating fried chicken covered with dust from sitting on the altar for seven days. Min Min doesn't see. The lovesick boy wanders aimlessly and pays no attention to anyone. His sleepless eyes look everywhere for her. Where can Pan Nyo be? From which direction will he hear her broken-hearted singing?

Pan Nyo's family is not at the rest house. They're not anywhere. Pan Nyo is gone, run away because she detests cheats. The tender girl he hurt with his lies. The child in him wants to cry, right in the middle of the main festival lane. How many times has he circled the fairgrounds? How many times does he call out, *Pan Nyo?*

Min Min feels feverish. He can't keep his balance. He collapses against the corner post of a hut and tosses his head back with eyes closed. Mustn't be so delicate, not if he's going to lift heavy loads for a living or pedal a trishaw. Where are you, Pan Nyo?

*Oh, that's just Daisy Bond's husband, Min Min. Must be drunk.*

Who's talking about him? Calling him Daisy Bond's husband? Min Min props himself up against the post. Nothing but *meinmashas*. Don't even want to look. Got to get out of here, away from U Ba Si's spies. Whatever happens to me is nobody's business. He's street scum now. No fancy boy that Daisy keeps, just a hungry scavenger now. If he ever finds Pan Nyo, he'd beg her for some of her begged rice. His belly is so empty it hurts.

Got to sleep somewhere. Min Min walks and walks, his fever rises, the *nat* music ringing in his ears. He'll look for Pan Nyo again tomorrow. The day after the full moon there's a communal alms-giving for the monks at the Wish-Fulfilling Pagoda. Then a "leftover ceremony" where the temple gives away the piles of excess food offerings and bananas to anyone in need. Madame Hassle attends the ceremony every year, as do beggars. He just hopes the sad girl will show.

Must lie down somewhere. Min Min's mind drifts off, leading his footsteps somewhere he knows. Past huts, turning here, along a fence, stopping at an arched gate with red bougainvilleas. His eyes don't want to open, but he can see it. Min Min falls down, relieved, oblivious to everything.

Who's this calling *Darling Min*? Has Pan Nyo been worrying about him? Please don't cry, Pan Nyo, Big Bro wants to lay his fevered brow on your cheek.


THE AUGUST breeze bids farewell as a long line of cars inches down the Taungbyon Road. Leaving in a white Toyota Hi-Lux, Daisy anxiously hugs his beloved young Min Min, weak and feverish on his lap. Again and again he prays to the

Buddha and beseeches the two Lords, *Make him well, rid him of all illness. Don't let him die, give me his sickness instead. I'm old, I've lived long enough.*

The roofed pickup slows to a stop at the railway crossing gate. Daisy turns around to see that Ahpongyi is in back and everything is okay. If Min Min were well, he'd be standing on the rear bumper, looking after things so the Bond Girl could sit pretty in the front seat.

Daisy looks at Min Min again with womanly care, when a sudden train whistle startles Min Min and throws him into a tizzy. Go back to sleep, it's nothing, nothing. Now the blue Taungbyon–Mandalay local rattles across, packed with people and *nat* images, and a lone voice pines amidst all the noise.

> *. . . To whom it may concern*
> *I send my love and yearn*
> *For your swift and safe return . . .*

Min Min shakes all over. His hazy eyes blink open, his dry lips mouth *Pan Nyo*.

> *. . . I parcel out my heart and care*
> *It may take months may take years . . .*

He struggles to squirm free of Daisy's arms. "She's . . . on the train."

Daisy hugs him, he's shivering. It's just a fever dream. Sleep, just sleep.

Did he imagine Pan Nyo? Wasn't that her voice? It must

have been. Weak and depressed, Min Min closes his eyes as the pining voice fades away and is gone.

> . . . *After all*
> *So far, so long*
> *Will you recall*
> *My voice, my song* . . .

ACKNOWLEDGMENTS

I would like to thank the many people who made this publication possible: my translator friends Ma Thi Thi Aye and Ko Yè Lin (Alfred Birnbaum), who actively sought out a receptive publishing house in the West; editors Will Schwalbe and Chisomo Kalinga and everyone at Hyperion who believed in the project; the late U Soe Kyi, my substantive model for Daisy Bond, as well as the many other *natkadaw* mediums of Taungbyon; and of course my husband, Aung Kyaw Toe, who has accompanied me every step of the way. May the Spirits smile on you all.